"It's not a mansion, but it meets my needs."

Serena could feel Andrew's eyes on her as she took in the view of his apartment, but he didn't try to interrupt her. His scrutiny made her neck feel warm.

Serena smiled, her flush creeping higher. "It looks great." The simple awareness of him made her so uncomfortable that she scanned the room again for a distraction. Her gaze caught behind the door on a Harley-Davidson poster that seemed so out of character for the stereotypical youth minister she'd created in her mind. She got the feeling there was more to Andrew Westin than she'd originally guessed....

Books by Dana Corbit

Love Inspired

A Blessed Life #188

DANA CORBIT

has been fascinated with words since third grade, when she began stringing together stanzas of rhyme. That interest, and an inherent nosiness, led her to a career as a newspaper reporter and editor. After earning state and national recognition in journalism, she traded her career for stay-at-home motherhood.

But the need for creative expression followed her home, and later through the move from Indiana to Milford, Michigan. Outside the office Dana discovered the joy of writing fiction. In stolen hours, during naps and between carpooling and church activities, she escapes into her private world, telling stories from her heart.

Dana now makes her home in Grand Rapids, Michigan, with her husband, three young daughters and two cats.

A Blessed Life
Dana Corbit

Published by Steeple Hill Books™

STEEPLE HILL BOOKS

Steeple
Hill™

ISBN 0-373-87195-3

A BLESSED LIFE

Copyright © 2002 by Dana Corbit Nussio

Visit us at www.steeplehill.com

Printed in U.S.A.

Cast your burden on the Lord,
and He will sustain you;
He will never permit the righteous to be moved.
—*Psalms* 55:22

Dedicated to the little angels of my heart,
Marissa, Caterina and Alexa—especially to Caterina,
whose painful journey inspired this story. Also to
Randy, who makes me believe in miracles.

A special thanks to GDRWA and MMRWA
members, for endless support; to Melissa Baxter,
for always believing; and to Dr. Celia D'Errico,
D.O., and Dr. Hilary Haftel, M.D.,
for your answers and for your hope.

Prologue

The waiting room stretched for miles in shades of warm tan and cheery peach, with pastel ocean scenes dotting the walls.

Every bit of it was a lie.

There was nothing sunny or happy about sitting in this sanitized holding cell. Not when Serena would have given anything to be on the other side of the wall...with Tessa. Instead she was forced to wait in here, helpless, while someone jammed a needle into her daughter's hip, examining the bone marrow there, looking for the worst.

"If this is a charmed life, I'd sure hate to see a cursed one." Serena didn't care if the other parents and grandparents in the room overheard her mumbling. She squeezed her eyes shut but could still see her little girl, so far from her arms. At least the three-year-old was slumbering away her mother's desertion and the medical assault on her body.

Unable to sit any longer, Serena stood and stretched her stiff legs, pacing the length of the room. She passed the television screen that had switched from a morning talk show to the midday news. Even the smell of this place—stale chips and soda—added to the nausea that had been building since this morning when she'd brought Tessa for her bone marrow biopsy—alone.

She stared by turns at the pay phone and her watch. Where was Trent? He'd promised to be here. This time at least...if none of the others. As frustrating as it was to admit, she knew if he walked through the door that minute, she'd forgive him for everything. For every time he'd failed her and their daughter since Tessa first became ill. Even for the indiscretions she suspected. If he'd be a stand-up husband just this once, she'd find a way to work through the rest of their problems. Finally, she gave in and dialed.

"Deirdre, this is Serena Jacobs again. May I speak to Trent?"

"I'm sorry, Mrs. Jacobs. Mr. Jacobs still isn't in. I checked his schedule, and he'd planned to be out most of the day. Is there a message I can give him when he calls in?"

"Yes, please tell him I'm still waiting at the hospital." She hung up the phone without waiting for the pleasantries.

Shuffling back to the upholstered chair she'd claimed as hers, she wrapped her sweater tightly around her shoulders. Outside, the July heat had turned southeast Michigan into a steam bath, but here inside, she was chilled to the bone. She fought the fog that was clouding her vision, but the tears came anyway, dampening her face before she could grasp for control.

Trent, please show up. Tessa needs you. I need you.

Serena pulled a tissue from her purse and dabbed at her eyes, ending up with a soggy tissue that had done nothing to stem the flow. Glancing up, she caught the other people in the waiting room trying not to stare.

She had to get control of herself. It would terrify Tessa if she saw her mother looking as if she'd just come from a funeral. In many ways she had, but that didn't matter. Not now. Tessa needed strength from her parents, at least from the one who wouldn't fail her. She straightened in her seat and rubbed her thumb along her lash line, clearing the smudged eyeliner.

No matter what the hematology oncologist told her today, she planned to stay strong for Tessa's sake. Leukemia was an unlikely diagnosis; the physicians had made that much clear. They were only ruling out the last of the "ugly" diseases before they could trust their earlier suspicions. And those weren't all that beautiful themselves.

Please, God, let it only be JRA. She stared at the floor, keeping her eyes open for fear she would pass out if she shut out the light. Her stomach clenched and sweat gathered under her bangs. What was she

saying? Had she lost her mind? She shook her head.
Here she wasn't just hoping, but begging, that Tessa
would have to live with a potentially crippling
chronic illness like juvenile rheumatoid arthritis.
How could she wish that on her own child?

But that answer was as simple as that most wonderful word she kept repeating like a mantra: *life*.
No matter how difficult a diagnosis of JRA was, it,
unlike several of the diseases the specialists had
ruled out in the past few months, was something
Tessa could live with. Recent medical advances
even made it possible for her to have a high quality
of life. Serena realized she didn't have the luxury of
worrying about levels of contentment yet. When she
straightened, a renewed strength filled her.

"Mrs. Jacobs?" The anesthesiologist stood before
her, waiting until she looked up. "Tessa's in Phase
One Recovery, which means she's still sleeping, but
I'll go ahead and allow you into the PACU—that's
the post-anesthesia care unit—if you'd like to wait
with her."

When she reached the unit, Tessa was lying very
still in the hospital bed, looking even tinier than
when the anesthesiologist had taken her away. Her
need to make physical contact with her child was so
strong that Serena leaned over and brushed the mass
of dark curls from Tessa's forehead. She traced the
line of thick lashes resting against the child's cheek.
Tessa started, showing she was returning to consciousness.

Serena pulled her chair close to the bed, leaned

her head against the rail and poked her arms through
the bars, simply to touch her daughter's hand. She
should not have allowed the doctors to take Tessa
away. A better mother would have insisted, no matter what the hospital's ridiculous rules, on being allowed in the operating room.

She might have been too numb to fight earlier,
but she had to scratch her way out of this void now.
Tessa needed her. That was the important thing.

Staring down at her little girl, Serena felt the lul-
laby they sang together each night come from somewhere deep inside her. "Hush-a-bye, don't you cry,
go to sleep, my little baby. When you wake, you
will have all the pretty little horses." She wanted to
sing away all of the pain and the broken promise
that she'd always protect Tessa.

The child awoke in slow, groggy increments,
moaning as she returned from that dark place of un-
natural sleep.

"Hi, angel-cookie. Mommy's here." Serena used
the singsong voice that had always calmed her
daughter's bad dreams until now. But those visions
had been only of monsters that inhabited closets or
toys that made mischief. She wasn't at all sure she
had any remedy for Tessa's very real nightmares
today.

"Do you want Mommy to hold you?" She took
that moan as a "yes" and lifted Tessa from the bed,
wrapping her in a thin white blanket. The child's
gown was still unsnapped from when it had been

removed for surgery, so Serena carefully closed the fasteners while she held Tessa close.

Serena had no idea how many minutes or hours had passed—only that she'd been exactly where she needed to be—by the time the hematology oncologist took the other seat in the curtained cubicle. Tessa had become more coherent but was crabby and was fighting against her bunny hospital gown. Her mother calmed her with touch and kept rocking.

"Has my husband checked in with you?" The question seemed to be her last defense, as it delayed the verdict a few seconds more. Could she live with the answer the doctors had tried so hard to find? She had to. Tessa would need her now more than ever.

"I'm sorry, Mrs. Jacobs. We haven't heard from him, although we asked the waiting room volunteers to send him in when he arrives." She smiled with a comforting expression that tinged a bit too much on pity. "I do, however, have some good news for you."

Good news? Serena's heart rate must have tripled. Her oxygen supply seemed to be temporarily blocked. While questions whirled through her mind, she was able to choke out just two words. "Excuse me?"

"The bone marrow biopsy shows that your daughter does *not* have leukemia."

Chapter One

⌒

Twelve months later

Coming here had been a really bad idea. Turning around and heading home sounded like a perfect one. Serena hesitated a second longer before climbing the last two steps leading into Hickory Ridge Community Church. Once inside the heavy, twin glass doors and past the sanctuary, she headed up the stairs toward Andrew Westin's office.

What had she been thinking when she'd set up this appointment last week? Why had it sounded so much better to visit with a youth minister? Even one who, because of his training as a clinical counselor, frequently met with church members to discuss problems. This way, though, she had not been forced to admit, even to herself, that she was going to a shrink.

Right now, the anonymity of a private counseling

relationship sounded preferable by loads. If her parents were still living, or even if she'd developed some close friendships in her twenty-eight years, she wouldn't be in this position. Then she would have had someone to talk to. More useless "what ifs." What good had they done her so far?

Pushing forth with more confidence than she felt, she knocked on the door, hoping the youth minister had forgotten about the whole thing. Then she could forget to reschedule, and all would be well.

"It's open," said a baritone voice behind the door.

She shrugged. Well, at least the meeting was cost free. She used that thought to bolster her courage as she opened the door, plastering a smile on her face.

"Mr. Westin, I'm Serena Jacobs. We talked on the phone." She crossed the room with her right hand outstretched, but he stood and met her halfway. Out of his usual Sunday costume of a dark suit, he was dressed in jeans and a beige polo shirt that offset his tan.

"Call me Andrew, Mrs. Jacobs. 'Mr.' makes me feel old."

He gripped her hand with a firm shake that was just shy of painful. At five foot eight, Serena wasn't accustomed to having to look up to anyone, but Andrew's height of well over six feet forced her to lift her head to meet his gaze. He smiled down at her, though, and she found it easy to smile back.

It was the first time she'd seen Andrew up close, instead of across the church sanctuary where he and the Reverend Bob Woods sat, so she was surprised at how quickly he put her at ease. He probably had to take a whole class on that in his training for the ministry.

He sat in his upholstered executive chair, motioning for her to take the chair opposite the desk. Funny, he didn't much fit the picture she had of a member of the pastoral staff, even if he wasn't the church's head minister. His sandy brown hair was a tad too long, threatening to curl at his nape. And his dress was too casual for a game of golf, let alone for what she'd come to expect of a church leader.

She lowered herself into the armless visitor's chair. "Call me Serena. Mrs. Jacobs doesn't...fit anymore."

"Oh, I'm sorry. I wasn't aware you were... divorced?" The way he stressed the last word made it a question. The sadness in his gold-colored eyes appeared genuine.

She nodded. "It was final just last week." With nervous tension weighing on her and making it difficult for her to sit still, she looked about the room, conscious how plain it was. There were no pictures on the wall, short of Andrew's Master of Divinity degree. The dark paneling shone with a recent waxing, but still it held no warmth. Even his desk was surprisingly clear of clutter, personal or work-related. No pictures of the girlfriend back home, of parents, a kid brother or even a Labrador retriever. It was odd to be opening her personal life to someone who didn't seem to possess one himself.

"And that's the reason for your visit?"

Another statement-question. She would get really annoyed if he kept that up. "No, I'm handling that fairly well—as well as anybody can handle failure."

He didn't respond immediately, but must have swallowed hard because his Adam's apple jerked. She wondered if he had choked back a retort about her divorce.

"Then, what brings you here today?" Andrew leaned forward on his desk and steepled his fingers in a thoughtful pose. "I'm guessing from the way you always slip out the back door so quickly on Sunday mornings that it's not to get to know your pastoral staff better." One side of his mouth tipped up in a smirk, but his eyes twinkled to soften it.

A chuckle was out before she realized it was building. How long had it been since she'd laughed about anything aside from some of Tessa's antics? It felt good, really good. "You guessed right."

"Why don't you give me a break and tell me what I can do to help you. I'm trained as a counselor and a youth minister, but I'm terribly under-qualified as a mind reader."

Serena nodded and gathered all of her courage into a tight ball before tossing out, "I can't seem to shake this depression."

"Divorce will do that."

"No," she said, shaking her head so hard her neck ached. "The divorce isn't what's causing it, at least not all of it. My daughter's condition is just getting to me. She has juvenile rheumatoid arthritis.'' There. She'd said it. Strange how even admitting her depression aloud felt better than the guilt of keeping what she considered her selfish little problem bottled inside.

"I don't recognize that one. Can you tell me a little about it?''

"JRA is a chronic illness where the patient's body attacks her joints. There are three types of JRA. Only systemic-onset JRA—the rarest one and the type that Tessa has—can also affect internal organs.''

"What would that mean for her future?''

Serena leaped off into the rote speech that she used whenever anyone asked for details. If she kept it exactly the same—didn't change a single word in her dialogue—she promised herself, it would feel no more personal than a memorized poem. Rather than a description of agony.

"In extremely rare cases, JRA can cause severe crippling and blindness, but we try not to think about those things.'' She took a deep breath, trying to slow her racing heart. "With proper medication, most kids do very well. In fact, seventy percent go into permanent remission by the time they're adults.''

"That must give you so much hope. How did you recognize that something was wrong?''

"It started about a year and a half ago when she began to have fevers every day—really high fevers that never turned to the flu or colds.'' She folded her hands in her lap, trying hard not to wring them.

"Whenever Tessa had them, she'd also get this rash on her hands. Fevers and rash are symptoms only seen with systemic JRA. It wasn't until months later that she started having hot, swollen joints—the true arthritis."

Andrew nodded. "You've been through quite an ordeal."

"Not me. My little girl." This was a mistake. She shouldn't have come here. Talking about it wasn't helping at all. It was only making her feel worse. "The illness itself is not the half of it. There were six months where the doctors didn't know for sure what was wrong with her."

She waited for Andrew to speak, to ask questions, but he only nodded for her to continue.

"They tossed around words like *tumor, leukemia, tuberculosis and lupus.*" With each word, the memories flashed through her mind more clearly. The screams from so many needle pokes. The fear in her child's eyes that Serena couldn't soothe. "She went through all kinds of tests—chest X rays, a ton of blood work, ultrasounds. They even tested her bone marrow for leukemia. We didn't know for a long time if she would…live or die."

The last was too much for her. A sob escaped her, though she tried with all her strength to hold it in. It wasn't like her to lose control. She was usually better at keeping it all boxed in. But this time she couldn't stop the tears from raining down her cheeks.

Andrew pushed a box of tissues to within her

reach. When she looked up at him, he shook his head slowly. "And you wonder why you're depressed? Look at all you've been through—not just your daughter, but you. The fear, the pain, the frustration. Not to mention a divorce, no matter how well you're handling it. All of that adds up to some very explainable blues."

She crossed her arms to hug away a chill, despite the July heat pouring through Andrew's open window. "But it doesn't make any sense. She was diagnosed a year ago. She's even doing a little better lately. So why am I depressed now? Why not when she was going through all of the tests, when we had no idea what was wrong? Why not right after the diagnosis?"

Andrew shrugged. "Some people operate in crisis mode. During the most difficult times of their lives they simply handle whatever is happening without really sitting back to analyze it." He leaned his elbows on the desk and rested his chin in the cradle of his palms. "It's only when things are better that they can allow themselves to collapse under the weight."

As if a lock suddenly had been fitted with a key, she felt a freeing *click* inside. "Maybe that's what I've done."

"Maybe. As well as all of the other changes in your life, haven't you also just moved?" He waited for her nod. "Why did you pick Milford?"

"It's fairly close to Ann Arbor, so I could take Tessa to C.S. Mott Children's Hospital at the University of Michigan. There are only a few hospitals with pediatric rheumatologists on staff.'' Her sacrifice had been small when she thought of the pain that Tessa faced daily.

"Did you find work here?"

"I'm a freelance writer. With a modem and my stable of regular contacts, I can live anywhere. Besides, Milford is such a quaint little village. And it's clear across the state from my former husband and his new bride.''

He chuckled. "You've had so many changes in such a short period. Until now, you've hardly had the time to be depressed. Now that your world has slowed, you're having these feelings, and I'm glad you're talking about them. That will help a lot.''

Was there some neat little order that these feelings could fall into, like dividers that create order in a junk drawer? Somehow she doubted it. No, for once she was positive about something. It would never be that simple.

"I just feel so guilty.'' She buried her face in her hands, allowing the blame to cover her like a dark, scratchy blanket. Seconds ticked by as she tried to tuck the feelings back into compartments where she could face them again. "For not being a stronger parent, for not being able stop Tessa's pain, but, most of all, for mourning the loss of my perfect daughter—our perfect life.''

Andrew planted both hands on the desk, then lowered them and rocked in the chair. His actions confused her.

"What do you mean, perfect?" He pressed a crooked index finger to his lips.

She chuckled at both herself and his counselor's pose. "I know it sounds silly, but I used to believe I led a charmed life. I had a good home, a nice family—everything anyone could ask for. And then the whole thing fell apart. Tessa got sick, and Trent cheated on me and left me for someone else. No more charmed life."

He studied her for several seconds. "I wish I had met you several years ago."

To her humiliation, the skin on her arms began to tingle. She couldn't allow herself to consider how meeting a nice guy like him years earlier might have changed her life. She rubbed her damp palms down her skirt, resisting the urge to smooth her blouse, as well.

"Why is that?" She choked out the words.

"Because this is what I would have said to you then—'You believe your life is charmed? Just wait, because nobody gets out of here free.'"

Serena chuckled. How right he was. "And I wouldn't have bought a bit of it back then. It's only now that I would have realized you were a genius."

"If we've just met and you think I'm a genius, then we'd better avoid getting to know each other better. I'd hate to see my I.Q. plummet in your mind."

She laughed again, a real, honest laugh that felt wonderful. And to think that lately she'd wondered if she would ever laugh again. He was so easy to talk to. And he made her feel as if everything was going to be all right—for the low, low price of free.

Andrew tapped his fingers on his desk a few times until she finally looked back at him. "It's okay to feel sad, you know. About Tessa's illness. About the divorce. Even about the loss of your charmed life."

"Then, why do I feel so guilty about being sad?"

"This is just a guess, but I think you're used to being in control. You haven't been able to control any of these things, and it's making you crazy."

She raised an eyebrow. "Crazy? Is that a word a counselor should be using?"

"I'm a youth minister these days. I've forgotten all of those rules."

"So I'm supposing you'll be recommending me to *real* counselors now?" She'd done it—used a sentence as a question. Great, now she was talking like him.

He shook his head. "So you're having a bit of a pity party after a really rough year and a half. Who could blame you? I'm not saying never to seek professional help, but you probably could wait for a while. Treat yourself really well and wait to see if the blues subside. If not, then seek further help."

"Is that your professional advice, *Mr.* Westin?" She stood to indicate she was ready to leave.

"Absolutely, *Mrs.* Jacobs." He followed her to the door. "Now let's discuss that little matter of payment."

Serena looked over her shoulder at him and

chuckled. "I gave at the office—I mean, in the offering plate."

"Oh, well then. See you Sunday."

Andrew closed the door on his most nerve-
racking day since starting his fellowship at Hickory
Ridge Community Church six months earlier. Had
she noticed that he'd swallowed hard every time she
pushed her shiny, dark hair behind her ears, letting
the sun dance on its auburn highlights? He'd thought
she was beautiful, having only seen her from across
the church. But up close, she was amazing.

At least he'd known enough the past few Sundays
to be glad it was Reverend Bob's job to deliver the
sermon and not his. Otherwise, he was sure Paul's
admonishment to the church at Corinth would have
been full of warnings about long, wavy hair and full
lips.

Now that he'd had a good look at her, the image
in his head this Sunday would be more vivid. He
would see eyes that were a combination of delica-
cies—shaped like almonds and the hue of dark chocolate. He would know that her face was a little too
square, her nose too straight, to earn her the title of
classic beauty, but that somehow made her more ap-
pealing. He couldn't allow himself to think about
the way she looked in her prim white blouse and
that skirt/shorts thing, even now, without breaking a
sweat.

It would surely require a prayer for forgiveness,
but he'd been thankful when he'd learned she was

divorced. It should have made him want to step back from her, but it didn't.

Pushing those dangerous thoughts away, Andrew pulled the monthly youth calendar up on his computer screen. Immediately, he felt tired. In theory, it was great to keep the youth too occupied in the summer to get into trouble, but all of those activities required chaperoning. The finger for that job pointed right back at him.

Trips to the Detroit Zoo and Michigan's Adventure Park in Muskegon, plus pizza night—that would be enough without tonight's youth lock-in. That was all he needed—spending twelve hours in a house full of adolescents. Eating too much junk food. Getting no sleep. Even with reliable fellow chaperones Robert and Diana Lidstrom and Charlene Lowe, it would be a harrowing night.

He walked to the window and stared out across the field to the older farmhouse that served as both his home and the temporary Family Life Center. The deacons had been fortunate that the prior owner had been ready to retire to Florida when they'd searched for property on which to build a new center.

Architects were already planning the shiny, modern structure that would stand there after the house was razed, but as he looked at the existing building—majestic in its own utilitarian way—he wished they'd just leave it alone. It had such character. Such history. The house spoke to a time when Milford had been a farming area instead of a bedroom community for Detroit.

Twirling the blind control, Andrew darkened the room and returned to his desk, wondering why the old house was so important to him. No one had promised him a permanent job in Milford. He was still only in the ''hope'' phase. But if he could prove himself indispensable to the deacons here, maybe he could finally convince the naysayers in his life that he was at least a little worthwhile.

And maybe he could convince himself.

Another image of that willowy brunette became a castaway in his thoughts, making him more uncomfortable than he cared to admit. Even if this wasn't a true doctor-patient situation where he needed to avoid personal involvement. Obviously, it had been too long since he'd had a real date, if he was allowing their conversation to take on this much significance. He had to get out more. But a feeling deep in his gut made him wonder if he'd still be having these same unsettling feelings even if he'd had a month's worth of interesting dates.

The phone rang and saved him from the uncertain implications of his thoughts. He didn't need or want the complications of an involvement now. Especially not with a troubled woman. She had as many problems as he did.

''Hickory Ridge Church, this is Andrew Westin. May I help you?''

''Andrew, this is Charlene.'' She spoke in that heavy New Jersey accent that made her identification unnecessary. ''Got bad news. My mom's hav-

ing emergency gall bladder surgery. I hate to bail
out on you, but..."

"Of course, Char, you have to be with your mom.
Don't worry a bit about us. I'll find someone else
to fill in. Let your mother know we'll be praying for
her."

He lowered the phone to the receiver, feeling a
new weight on his shoulders. Did he know anyone
who was crazy enough—or naive enough, to agree
to chaperone a youth all-nighter with less than eight
hours' notice? A few faces flickered in his mind and
disappeared, but one unlikely image showed up and
refused to fade.

Chapter Two

Still digesting that unsettling meeting with Andrew Westin, Serena pulled her Ford Taurus station wagon to the curb. Their conversation wasn't going down easily. She needed more time to ponder it, but, as always, other needs came first.

"Hi Mommy," Tessa chimed, stepping cautiously down the front steps of their next-door neighbor's home with Mrs. Nelson at her heels. "We made chocolate chip cookies."

As if that wasn't obvious from the ingredients pasted to the front of her formerly pink T-shirt. "I bet that was a lot of fun. Thank you, Mrs. Nelson. For everything."

The feisty retiree rolled her lips inward to stifle a laugh. Despite the added laundry challenge, Serena was grateful her neighbor with an overbooked social calendar had been available to sit. Her appointment, and the resulting panicked search for child care, had reminded her how important it was to find a regular sitter.

"Can we go to the park, Mommy? Please?"

That pleading head tilt was the one that often worked on Serena. She was being played like a song, and she didn't mind the melody. A glance at her watch told her there was enough time to play awhile and have lunch before Tessa's nap.

"Okay, but let's change your shirt first."

Only fifteen minutes after their arrival at Central Park and its special playground, River Bend Playscape, Serena wondered why she'd even changed Tessa's clothes. She looked as if she'd lost a fight with a dust storm, but that impish grin showed she was an excellent loser. She sat wide-legged in the sandbox, having traded the cleaner play of digging with the permanent bulldozer contraption for the joy of sinking her bare feet in the sand.

Serena felt as happy as her daughter looked, here in this moment of no sickness, no visible pain. If she were honest with herself, she'd have to admit that she'd felt lighter ever since leaving Andrew's office—even if she was having a difficult time figuring out what to do with that weightlessness. His words had shown her a flash of light at the end of the dark tunnel that was her life.

"'Nobody gets out of here free.'" She repeated his words under her breath and grinned. If he'd said that to her two years ago, she would have laughed out loud at his bleak predictions. How had he come to know so much? He looked to be only a few years older than she was.

But somehow, talking to him had made her feel less alone in her misery. Did the comfort come from realizing everyone had pain, or from knowing that Andrew cared about hers? Answering that question would force her to analyze several of today's wayward thoughts, so she drew no conclusion.

Even if she were ready to consider a relationship again—which she wasn't—Andrew wouldn't have been her choice. He was a youth minister. In her wildest imaginings for the future, she'd never once pictured herself as a minister's wife. Those women wore buns in their hair and played church organs.

"What's so funny, Mommy?"

Serena looked at her sand sculpture of a daughter, embarrassed to have been caught in her musings. "I remembered a funny joke, honey."

Tessa raised a quizzical eyebrow in an expression destined in her teen years to be perfected into a smirk. "Can I play on the slides?"

Swallowing the knot of anxiety in her throat, Serena reminded herself that the doctors wanted Tessa to remain active. They promised Tessa would set her own limits, based on the pain, and Serena hoped they were right. "Which one do you want to try first?"

She need not have worried. Tessa was timid enough for the both of them. Serena took her position at the bottom of the play structure, watching her child amble instead of run across the polyvinyl-coated bridge toward the curly tube slide.

Serena caught her at the bottom. "Here, jump to the ground."

Tessa shook her head and lifted her arms. Serena's throat felt dry, and her eyes burned. But she would not cry. She couldn't allow that. She lifted her frail child, wondering if that fearless toddler, the one who had once scaled monkey bars and jumped off front porch steps instead of walking down, still existed. She had to be hidden in there somewhere. The same way Tessa's puffy cheeks and swollen belly—side effects of her steroid medications—merely covered the healthy child beneath.

Serena shook away her sadness over their losses. Mourning didn't do a bit of good. Besides, there was so much to be thankful for. Tessa's skin no longer carried that ghostly pallor of anemia, meaning the medication was doing something. And the new medicine had helped so many other children. Hopefully it would have the same success with Tessa's condition.

When her child crawled up in her lap as she sat on the bench, Serena knew it was time to go home. Exhaustion often hit hard, making daily naps necessary. She fastened Tessa into her car seat and drove home for what was always the hardest part of the day. "Quiet time" left Serena with too many minutes alone with her thoughts. Like usual, she'd spend most of it feeling sorry for herself.

* * *

She barely had time to tuck Tessa into bed and kiss her the pre-ordered three times, before the phone rang. A freelance career wasn't always what it was marketed to be. What sounded like freedom often turned into career captivity when your home was your office. Sometimes she wished she could turn off the phone and hide until she was ready to do business again, but she couldn't afford to lose any clients, especially now that she was a single parent. Her freelance income paid the rent.

"Serena Jacobs. May I help you?" It was a funny way to answer her home phone, but lately, her calls were more often business than personal.

"Hi, Serena. It's Andrew Westin."

She swallowed hard. What if he'd reconsidered his advice this morning and wanted to suggest that she seek counseling as soon as possible? "Hello, Andrew..." Not sure what to say, she hoped he would fill in the gap.

"It was good meeting you today."

"Nice meeting you, too," she mumbled, her nervousness growing exponentially.

"I've been thinking a lot about your situation, being down in the dumps."

She took a deep breath. *Here it comes.* Maybe he was going to suggest something even worse, like she wasn't stable enough to care for Tessa. When he hesitated longer than she could handle, she prompted, "Yes?"

"One way to get out of depression is to get involved in helping someone else."

She smiled into the receiver, feeling silly over her worries. "And just who did you have in mind?"

"Me." Andrew paused. "And about thirty of my closest friends."

Trying hard not to be flattered, she waded through his words, searching for some deeper meaning. Was this his roundabout way of asking her out? If it were, what would she answer?

"Are you still there? I just asked if you'd ever worked with kids."

Serena brushed her hand back through her wind-tangled hair and blushed, glad he couldn't see her. Obviously, she was letting her imagination get the best of her.

"I taught toddler Sunday School for about a year after I graduated." Why did she feel like she was being hooked here like a bad act in a variety show— only she was being dragged out *onto* the stage, not off.

"Perfect." He made a sound into the receiver as if he'd snapped his fingers. "Then, I have just the job for you—chaperone for tonight's teen lock-in."

"Oh, I don't really—"

"Please, before you say no, hear me out."

She had no business even thinking about volunteering for something like this. Her focus needed to always be on Tessa. Still, it would be rude not to at least give the youth minister a chance to explain. "Go ahead."

His words came out in a rush, blending excitement and desperation. "Well, you see, there's this lock-in tonight. It will be about thirty kids, from seventh to twelfth grades. They play board games, have organized activities, listen to clean music, watch approved videos and eat junk food.''

She carried the phone into her bedroom, past the bed and dresser that were pressed so closely together she could barely open the drawers. When she reached her messy desk by the window, she sat and pushed through the pile of works in progress.

''Yes, I know what a lock-in is. We had them all the time in our youth group.''

''Well, the special thing about this particular lock-in is that it's my *first* one as youth minister. I thought I had the whole thing under control, with four chaperones—myself included—lined up. Only, Char had a family emergency, and I haven't been able to find a replacement.''

''How many people have you asked before me?''

''About a dozen.''

She smiled into the receiver. ''Glad to hear I was your first choice. What did the first twelve say?''

''They pretty much wished me the best in finding someone who was…available.''

''Then, I'll have to do the same, I think.''

''Are you saying you're not available?''

She could feel the tightrope swaying beneath her toes. Could she decline carefully without lying? ''I never said that. But I do have one small complication—a four-year-old one. I'm new here. I don't have any regular baby-sitters for Tessa, even if I could get someone on such short notice.''

"I wonder what would have happened if Simon, Peter and Andrew had been too busy casting nets on the Sea of Galilee to follow Jesus so he could make them 'fishers of men.'"

"That's not quite fair."

"I'm just kidding. If you're willing to chaperone, you're more than welcome to bring Tessa. She'll be the hit of the party. And later we can put her to bed in my room."

"I still don't think—"

He continued as if she hadn't spoken. "Hey, if you're looking for baby-sitters, this is the place to be."

An overnight party, filled to the walls with potential baby-sitters—what could be the harm in that? She shook her head and stared out the lace-curtained window, glancing down at the street lined with old elms and maples.

She wasn't really considering this, was she? It would take no more than one hand to enumerate the things she knew about teenagers, and at least four of those things she'd learned while living through that misery herself.

"I just don't think it would be the best idea—"

"Do you think I'd be calling you—a new attendee, not even a church member yet—if I weren't desperate? I have all these kids coming and not enough adults to chaperone. If you say no, I guess I'd better cancel the whole thing." He sighed. "Please, Serena. You're my last resort."

"Since you put it that way…"

"Thanks, Serena. You're a lifesaver."

As she hung up the phone, she couldn't help wondering if she was also a daredevil. Being in close proximity to Andrew Westin was probably not in her best interest. But for some reason, she couldn't resist.

Andrew opened the front door to the temporary Family Life Center and led Serena and Tessa into a huge, nearly empty room. Funny, he almost wished the space had a matched living room group and heavy draperies instead of mini-blinds on the windows and folding chairs stacked against the wall. "This is our main gathering place. We meet here on Sunday mornings for singing and prayer before Sunday School and again for youth group on Sunday nights."

"Doesn't anybody use it during the week?" Serena looked about, seeming less than overwhelmed by the old house's decor.

"Sure. Tuesday morning Bible study. The monthly men's breakfast. The Christian women's group. The church quilters. It's almost always in use."

"Didn't you say you live here?"

He nodded over his shoulder as he strode toward the kitchen. "I only use part of it. Hey, Tessa. Want to see the rest of the house?"

He looked back to see the child timidly investigating each room. The resemblance between the dark-haired pixie and her mother was amazing. She would be beautiful when she grew up. Although she'd been opening and closing the dining room blinds, when he spoke, Tessa accepted his hand and went with him to the kitchen.

"Mommy, there's a refrigerator…and a stove."

Serena watched the two of them—already buddies—feeling more relaxed than she had in weeks. Maybe volunteering was a good idea, after all.

"You're right. Do you think there might be dishes in those cabinets?"

"Let's see—" Tessa jerked the first door open. "Just pans." The disappointment in her voice made both adults grin.

Andrew scooped Tessa up in his arms as if he'd done it every night of her life, whirling her about the room and stopping before each upper cabinet door so she could look inside. "They're probably not as pretty as your mom's dishes, but they work okay for me."

"For you?" Tessa stopped opening doors long enough to look down at him. "Is this your house?"

He nodded. "Want to see my room?"

"Where is it?" She was already squirming to get out of his arms and investigate.

He pointed to the closed door off the kitchen. "There." He fished a key out of his pocket and laid it in Tessa's hand. She'd reached the lock, worked it and turned the knob before the grown-ups caught up with her.

Through the open doorway, Serena saw a small-ish, blue-carpeted bedroom that had been converted to an apartment of sorts. On one wall was a roughly constructed wooden loft bed with a plaid recliner and end table beneath it. Both faced a little TV balanced on milk crates.

On the opposite wall was a set of floor-to-ceiling bookshelves, built with the same primitive materials as the loft. The shelves were loaded, most of them stuffed two books deep. No more than three feet from the loft was a card table and chairs—a makeshift dinette.

Serena could feel Andrew's eyes on her as she took in the details, but he didn't try to interrupt her. His scrutiny made her neck feel warm.

"It's not a mansion, but it meets my needs."

She smiled, feeling the flush creep higher. "It looks great." The simple awareness of him made her so uncomfortable that she scanned the room again for a distraction. Her gaze caught a Harley-Davidson poster behind the door that seemed so out of character for the stereotypical youth minister she'd created in her mind. She got the feeling there was more to Andrew Westin than she'd originally guessed.

She glanced back to find him leaning against the door, his arms crossed in a casual pose. "It's really nice, but why don't you use the rest of the house?" she asked. As far as she could tell, the little bathroom, the kitchen and his multipurpose room formed his apartment in only one-quarter of the square footage.

He shrugged. "There's something about having my own space. You know what I mean?"

How odd that she did understand what he was saying. A few months ago she wouldn't have had a clue. Now it was clear. Personal space was about being in control—taking control—when the world all around was going crazy. She would have said that to him, or at least tried to relate the connection that she felt, if not for the crash that came from the other side of the house.

"Duty calls." He ushered them out of his room and turned the key before gesturing toward the locked door. "It never hurts to keep this room locked. It prevents the bed from mysteriously ending up short-sheeted and keeps my underwear from getting hung on the church flagpole. I wasn't born yesterday. Thirty-three years ago, to be exact." He headed toward the door. "We'd better greet the inmates."

Serena followed behind him, pulling a suddenly shy Tessa. Curious about his comment, Serena spoke to his retreating back. "Do you know that stuff from personal experience?"

He looked back at her over his shoulder, raising an eyebrow. She'd have to ask him about that later. She was pretty sure it would be a good story.

"All right, who banged the door?" he asked the crowd rushing through the entry.

A chorus of "not me" rang out, loud enough to rattle the shingles.

"Everyone, this is Serena and her daughter,

Tessa.'' He indicated the baker's dozen of teens already filling the living room. ''Serena, Tessa, this is everyone.''

A couple followed the kids through the door, their smiles as round as their middle-age waistlines. Assuming them to be the other two chaperones, Serena nodded to them, liking them on sight. She reached down to brush back her daughter's hair—Tessa had attached herself to her leg.

''And Serena and Tessa, I'd like you to meet Robert and Diana Lidstrom, the coolest soon-to-be grandparents east of Lake Michigan.'' Andrew gripped Robert's hand and planted a kiss on Diana's cheek in a single fluid motion. ''I wouldn't have considered tonight's adventure without them.''

Diana winked at Serena. ''We wouldn't have volunteered for just anybody, either. I think it was Kentucky's loss and Michigan's gain that Andrew ended up here.''

Serena turned to him. ''You're from Kentucky? You don't have the accent.''

He shrugged. ''It's Louisville. And I've worked hard to mask that accent.'' He said ''accent'' with an exaggerated Southern drawl.

Seeming not to notice the other adults around him, Robert dropped to a crouch to be eye-to-eye with Tessa. ''Hi, Tessa. Is this your first slumber party?''

Her shy nod led him to list the night's fun activities. Tessa released her grip on her mother's leg bit by bit, finally accepting Robert's outstretched hand and his offer to go find the potato chips.

Diana gestured toward their retreating backs. "It will be just like that when she grows up. Some boy's going to lead her away from you."

Serena shivered at the thought of that eventuality, reminding herself this was the normal course of things. She couldn't protect her daughter forever. "Don't remind me."

Diana patted her shoulder with a mother's sympathy. "Oh, that's *months* away from being a problem. How did Andrew twist your arm into being here tonight?"

"He bribed me with my choice of baby-sitters."

Diana winked knowingly. "I hope he didn't play on your sympathies and beg or anything."

Andrew whisked through the room, his arms loaded with pizza boxes. He returned from the kitchen a few minutes later with a slice in hand. "Guilty as charged. A desperate man, you know. Did what I had to in order to get what I needed."

Although he had spoken about her being a last-minute chaperone, the brief look he cast toward her made Serena wonder if there was something more to Andrew Westin's interest in her, more than his need for a volunteer. She could have sworn the ball of nerves rumbling inside her was from anticipation. And she knew better than to allow herself to feel that way.

But knowing was powerless against the hope that sprouted in her heart.

Chapter Three

"Go, horsey, go."

Tessa cracked a pretend whip on the shoulder of the make-believe stallion racing with her through the room. The equine creature more closely resembled a teenage girl with a long golden ponytail that bounced as she galloped. With a few waves and a whinny, horse and rider were off on another adventure.

"Giddy up, horsey, don't be slow. Take my Tessa to the rodeo."

Serena smiled, hearing her daughter repeat the rhyme they'd often say together. Tonight, her shy, clingy child of two hours before had transformed into the life of the party. The group's new mascot, Tessa already had played Ping-Pong, her head barely over the table, and had been on a team in the game of Life so she could get help collecting "paydays."

They had even let her pick the next contemporary Christian CD for the boom box.

It felt so good to see Tessa laughing, having fun, just like any normal child. Serena felt almost normal, too, and it seemed like a first gasp of fresh air after years of holding her breath.

"Did I mention a truckload of potential baby-sitters would be here?" Andrew asked from over her shoulder.

She shook off the tremor that his closeness produced and insisted that the hairs on the back of her neck lay down. This was ridiculous. She was a grown-up here, not one of the kids.

"Why do you think I'm here? Who is that with Tessa now?"

"Only seventeen-year-old baby-sitter extraordinaire, Hannah Woods." He turned to face Serena, watching her as if expecting her to react. "Think…Reverend Bob *Woods*."

The preacher's daughter. That couldn't hurt. It already was obvious that Hannah was great with children. This night was turning out to be more successful than Serena had expected. "Does she baby-sit a lot?"

"I'm sure she will for you, if you need her to."

Serena knew he was right. It was obvious Hannah adored Tessa. The two of them looked like old friends. Just seeing them together made Serena think about how nice it would be to get out of the house alone, once in a while, to run errands or grab a cup of coffee. Tessa would be in good hands.

"Hey, little cowgirl, do you need a fresh horse?" Andrew was already crouched low to prepare for a rider. "Your other one's wearing out."

A chair climb later, a successful exchange was made and they were off again, with Andrew in full trot. Seeing the two of them together tugged at Serena's heart, her thoughts bittersweet. How much did Tessa miss having a father in her life since Trent had deserted them both for that other woman?

Had her memories of her dad begun to fade? Serena certainly hadn't forgotten. It was just so much easier not to remember. As she watched Andrew and his rider, she remembered Tessa and Trent laughing together over a bathroom flooding with bubbles, and Daddy and daughter napping together on the sofa.

Tessa didn't ask questions about her father, at least not yet. What would Serena tell her when she did? Was there a gaping hole in Tessa's heart where a daddy should have been? Maybe someone like Andrew could fill that hole a little, or at least cover it with a bandage of compassion.

Watching the horse and his rider, Serena missed things she'd never had, longed for things she had no right to. Dreams emerged and danced off in various directions. She needed to shut away these thoughts before they led her to their only possible end—disappointment. She'd experienced enough of that to last a lifetime.

"Look at them go," Diana said, coming up behind Serena and patting her shoulder. "Andrew's such a doll. I'd do anything for him. He's going to be a wonderful father one of these days."

Serena stiffened. Was she so transparent that even an acquaintance could read her thoughts? How could she be considering only herself? She had no business entertaining selfish thoughts when Tessa needed to be her focus. What would happen if the JRA flared again? She couldn't allow any distraction from her duty to her child.

"Look who is queen of the mountain." Andrew approached, carrying Tessa on his shoulders. "Say something to your loyal subjects."

Serena reached up and rustled Tessa's already wild hair. "Better wave and turn over your scepter, sweetheart. It's time for you to go night-night." She prepared herself to have to drag away a kicking and screaming miniature queen, but Tessa climbed from one set of arms into the other and hugged her mom.

Tessa waved as Serena carried her through the house to the back bedroom that Andrew had unlocked. Once inside her Pooh sleeping bag, Tessa was asleep before they reached the last page of her bedtime story, but Serena read to the end, anyway. Brushing hair from her daughter's face, Serena dropped a kiss on her forehead and slipped from the room to return to the party.

Her exhausted body begged for a spot beside Tessa in that minuscule sleeping bag, but she'd made a commitment and she planned to follow through. Maybe she could convince a few of the youth to watch that *Charlie and the Chocolate Fac-*

tory video, so she could catch a few winks in the back of the room. *What a great idea.* Serena gave the shrill whistle that her mother had always called "unladylike."

"Thanks for the attention grabber, Serena," Andrew called from across the room. "It's nine-thirty. The party needs a fire built under it. Who wants to play Twister?"

It was well past noon by the time Andrew stared at his reflection in the bleary medicine cabinet mirror. It confirmed his suspicion. Even a Mack truck would have done a gentler makeover on his face. He should have slept like a baby after the last doughnut was munched and the last chip was sucked out of the carpet with the archaic vacuum.

But no, he just lay there in that pitiful square of a room, a series of still images flashing behind his eyelids in unending succession. Serena performing an award-worthy "parting of the Red Sea" clue in boys-versus-girls charades. Serena gathering that sweet little girl of hers into her arms in an embrace singularly shared between mothers and their children. Serena sneaking a look at him with what he couldn't help but interpret as attraction.

He smiled into the mirror. That was the way he wanted to interpret it. The message she wished for him to read was probably something else. Something with the words *Forget it* attached firmly at the end. No, the look was probably just gratitude for his helping her climb out of the dumps. She'd even smiled a few times tonight, although never at him. It was beautiful all the same.

With the Father's help, she could get through this difficult time in her life. She had only to ask for His help—something Andrew guessed was about the hardest thing ever for Serena to do. Why was it so important to him that she find her way? And why did he feel such a tug to be part of that path to discovery?

He yanked open the medicine cabinet and grabbed his toothbrush, not wanting to see that face in the mirror anymore. He couldn't allow himself to think of her this way. She was a divorcée—a recent one at that—with a child. It didn't matter at all to him, but he would have been naive not to realize some church members would consider a youth minister dating a divorcée to be scandalous.

Besides, Serena had so much baggage. Would he be able to handle helping her carry it? Of course, he knew better than to try. He'd even tasted the inevitable pain that an ill-advised relationship could cause. That knowledge, which had come courtesy of Marnie, had left a bitter taste in his mouth. The sting felt fresh sometimes, despite the few years' buffer since their breakup. He didn't want to feel pain like that ever again.

No, he could have no romantic fantasies about Serena Jacobs. His only interest in her should be spiritual. He sensed that she had a personal relationship with God, but it was obvious she wanted the Lord to take a hands-off approach, a plan that wasn't working well for her. Maybe his interest in her was God-sent, making him a vehicle for her spiritual guidance. That was all it could be.

Last night's party had given him an idea of a way to help Serena with her depression and to jump-start her spiritual growth at the same time. He shouldn't have to feel guilty that this ingenious plan—convincing her to teach Sunday School in the youth department—also happened to make his life a few hundred times easier, right? A knot that formed in his stomach made him wonder if regularly being that close to Serena, within reach but still so far away, wouldn't also make his life a lot harder.

Turning on the shower faucet, Andrew kept the water temperature a few degrees below comfortably warm. He shivered as he stepped under its spray and tipped his head back so the flood covered his face. This would be a good way to clear his mind of all unnecessary thoughts. Then he could focus on his calling to help the whole church community, not just one troubled young mother and her sick child. He hoped beyond hope that the water would also remove thoughts of dark, shiny hair and a sweet, feminine smile.

The knock had to be from miles away, somewhere in her dream, but it dragged Serena helplessly to consciousness, anyway. She heard the knock again, not ten feet from the sofa where she'd collapsed what seemed like only a few minutes before. She tried to lift up, but had to roll Tessa off her chest before she could move. How and when had Tessa gotten out of bed? She remembered putting her slumbering daughter to bed before giving in to exhaustion. At least, she thought she had.

Again the knock beckoned, louder this time. More insistent. Sitting up, she glanced at the wall clock in the corner. Three o'clock. Had they slept all day? She jogged to the front door and jerked it open. Andrew stood there, his hair damp and combed back straight, but his eyes looking anything but fresh. She steadied herself, refusing to acknowledge the immediate jolt to her system.

"It's about time. If I hadn't seen your car parked out front, I'd have given up and gone home."

She would have asked him why he was there in the first place, but his unusual demeanor hinted that he was wearing his minister's "hat" today. Something about this other side of him made her even less comfortable than did his presence as a man at her front door. She self-consciously patted down her hair, thankful that she'd been too tired to change out of her clothes when she'd arrived home. She was rumpled, but at least she was decent.

"I was trying to catch up on some much-needed rest. You might be able to relate." She pulled the door open wide. "Would you like to come in?"

She pushed the screen door halfway open and felt a whisk of air past her knees. Tessa, still wearing a pair of baby-doll pajamas, was in Andrew's arms before he made it through the front door. Immediately he slipped out of his official capacity and became Tessa's playmate, twirling her around and letting her drag him up the stairs to see her room.

Eventually, Tessa deserted her guest to go play "dress and undress" with her dolls, leaving Serena and Andrew to sit across from each other in the living room. The way he watched her today seemed more intense, as if he were looking straight into her soul. The knot in her belly felt as if it were pushing on vital organs. She wondered if he'd find her as vacant inside as she often felt.

"You had a nice time last night, didn't you?"

Relief flooded her. Maybe he would make this visit easy on her. "Yes, the kids were great. Tessa had a wonderful time. I'm glad we went."

He looked away, his gaze traveling over the navy-and-burgundy plaid sofa where he sat, then across the three-foot gap to the love seat she was perched on. "The kids were glad you were there, too. And they loved Tessa. You two really fit in."

She tried to forget her discomfort over what he must have thought about the cramped room, stuffed with furniture that had fit nicely in her old Grand Rapids home. Besides, the way he was talking made her uncomfortable.

"What are you getting at?"

"Have you ever thought about being involved with a youth group?"

"Not since I graduated from high school," she said with a quick smile.

"I mean as a teacher."

She raised an eyebrow at him. "Isn't that what the church pays you to do?"

He leaned forward, resting his elbows on his knees. "That's part of my job, but I'd like to have at least two Sunday School teachers for the youth department—one for junior high and one for high school. I'd take the high school class. Would you consider teaching the junior high class?"

"Oh, Andrew, I don't know about that."

"It would be really easy. The lessons are all broken down in the teacher's guide. If you have any other questions each week, I'm always available to help you. You'll feel so much better if you stay busy helping other people."

She shook her head. He wasn't playing fair. He was making it hard to say no. "That just doesn't seem like a good idea to me."

"Didn't you like the youth group when you were a teen?"

"I loved it."

"Then, I'm sure you want that same great experience for the kids here in Milford."

Serena chuckled. He should have been a politician. He already had persuasion down to an art. "Yes, I want that, but—"

"Did your parents bring you to church when you were little?"

What kind of new approach was this? She felt as if she were being manipulated, and wondered how to respond. "Every week. It was a real family affair."

"Did they force you to go?"

She shook her head. "No, never. I wanted to go. I was a teenager who looked forward to it. Does that sound strange to you?"

He threw his head back and laughed. "Not to me. I just want to know how they did it and how I can pass that information along to the parents of my kids."

His kids. She liked the way he claimed the church's youth as his own. "Their method was pretty simple. They introduced me to their loving God and helped me to develop a friendship with Him, as well." Vignettes from happier times filled her mind, full of her parents' smiles and songs of praise. "It was so easy to love the Lord then."

She was surprised that she'd spoken those words aloud.

He said nothing for a long time, then finally nodded. "That would be hard for me to understand if I hadn't experienced it myself, but I know what it's like to struggle with trusting God even when I need Him most."

She stared into eyes, her questions finding no answers in his carefully neutral gaze. He straightened, as if he recognized her awakening curiosity about his own box of secrets. She had a pretty good idea that he wouldn't give her a chance to pry.

"Now is your time to trust, Serena. The Father is waiting. You have only to ask." He spread his arms, hands palms up, as if to demonstrate the simplicity of his seemingly monumental request.

"Come on, Andrew. I've never said I lost faith. I still believe, just as I always have."

"What have you always believed? That God is this wonderful benevolent spirit who's there to make the daffodils bloom but can't be called upon for anything more complicated than traveling mercies or final exam support?"

"I don't think you're being fair."

"I'm sorry. I guess I'm not." Andrew shifted in his seat again, leaning forward. "I just want you to see that it's okay to give up the power, to allow God to carry you through times when you can't walk under your own steam."

Anguish gripped her in its powerful fist, but she fought for control. Always control. "You don't understand. I've had to walk alone too long. Too far."

"I'm sorry that your former husband hurt you. You never should have had to experience his betrayal. He failed you when you needed him. But God never did. And He never will."

The subject died a quick death then. She didn't want to reveal all of the humiliating details. Although she could hardly argue with his logic about God, she wasn't ready to inhale his words like the scent of lilacs, either. It was easier to let it drop.

The silence between them disturbing her, she returned to the earlier—safer—subject. "I really did have fun last night. Tessa did, too."

Andrew grinned, seeming to put behind him the intensity of the moment before. "She's great, you know."

"Yes, I know."

"So are you...especially with the youth group."

Her laugh started somewhere deep inside and bubbled out. She had to give him credit for trying. Besides, she had enjoyed working with the teens at the overnighter. Teaching Sunday School would be fun. Tessa would be in her Tiny Tots class, so it wasn't like Serena would be deserting her. Being needed wasn't so bad, either.

"Okay, I'll do it."

Andrew was out of his seat and in front of her before the fourth word left her mouth. He knelt and gripped both of her hands together between his. "Thank you. Thank you. You won't regret it."

But with the way her hands tingled, as if they were awakening from a numbing sleep, she had to wonder. She suspected that working with Andrew was going to be the best—or the worst—decision she'd ever made.

Chapter Four

Reverend Bob turned to another passage in his huge black Bible on Sunday morning, the flutter of pages amplified by the microphone.

"In the Book of John, did Jesus say to the woman at the well, 'You are a sinner, so I cannot look at you'? Or 'Because I am a Jew and you are a Samaritan, I cannot speak to you'?"

Murmurs of "no" popped up in the packed sanctuary.

"Not my Jesus," he said with a firm shake of his head. "Not my Lord who loves all us sinners. Instead He told her about His 'living water.' Shouldn't we aspire to our Lord's type of compassion? Let us all love our neighbors without falling to the temptation to judge."

Reverend Bob shut his Bible with a *snap*, startling Andrew in his seat just behind the minister's left shoulder. He hoped no one noticed how far his thoughts had been from the Samaritan woman and how close they were to the lady frowning in the back pew.

Serena obviously had been trying all through the service to keep her daughter quiet. Tessa couldn't have been that loud, or he would have heard her. But how could he have heard anything over the crinkling of candy wrappers, seventh-grade giggles, and what could only have been a snore elsewhere in the sanctuary?

Memories of his own childhood antics in church filtered through his mind—of crawling under pews, rustling hymnal pages and faking sneezes. And of spankings and more painful criticism after the services. Somehow, he felt certain Tessa's reprimand would be a loving one.

Heat scaled his neck, so he glanced to the other side of the auditorium, away from Serena, who sat ready to entrance him again. He steadied himself as he rose for the invitation. He had to get out of this service and into some private prayer where he could find perspective.

That goal helped him through the closing hymn. Only his regular stint in the greeting line remained; then he'd be free for a few hours until the evening youth group meeting. He pressed through the crowd, but two women became a solid wall of delay.

He pasted on his best smile and called for a heavenly gift of patience. "Hello, Mrs. Sims." He nodded to the elder before turning to the younger. "And Charity."

Laura Sims shook her index finger at him, making a clucking noise. "Now, Andrew Westin, you know you don't have to be so formal with me. You call me Laura, or at the very least, Sister Laura."

He nodded. "Of course, Laura. Did you ladies enjoy the service today?" It was so much easier to address the two of them jointly rather than speaking to Charity individually and risk accidentally encouraging her interest in him. That was the last thing he wanted to do.

Matchmaker Laura always seemed to be pushing her near-spinster daughter in her search for a suitable son-in-law. No matchmaking would have been necessary if Charity had possessed a sweet personality to match her trim figure, golden hair and green eyes. Frustration filled him that he continued to be prospect number one—all because he had chosen a career in the ministry.

Charity stepped forward. "I don't know about you, but I've always found the woman at the well story to be a difficult one. She was living in sin and everything. It would be so hard for me to…you know."

Andrew met Charity's gaze for the first time in the conversation, and the urge to grab her shoulders and shake her filled him. It was wrong, and he knew it. He should have been concerned with her spiritual growth, just as he was with Serena's. But her judgmental attitude got under his skin.

"Reach out to her, you mean? Didn't Christ set a great example of what we all should do?"

"That He did, Andrew. That He did." Laura patted Andrew's shoulder as if they were already related and she were relieving familial stress.

"I'd better get to the door. Reverend Bob is waiting for me." He hurried up the aisle, but most of the members had already gone outside, all except Serena and Tessa. Serena looked as though she were a reluctant captive in her conversation with the minister. Tessa seemed to be having a great time clanging coat hangers.

"Hey, Tess." He swung her up in his arms. "Were you having trouble sitting still in church?"

She shrugged, a mischievous look lighting her eyes. "I'm hungry."

He lowered Tessa, squatting before her and trying to keep a straight face. "I'm sure it's tough when you're hungry like that. But I bet it would make your mommy happy if you'd try to sit still and be quiet during the service. God would be real happy, too."

"Okay."

Okay. It was as simple as that to a child. Why did everything become so complicated for adults? Serena looked over at him, appearing grateful.

The glass door opened and Hannah popped in to relieve Andrew of his tiny charge. The two girls, one quite a few heads taller than the other, darted off hand-in-hand.

He wished someone like Hannah had taken him under her wing when he was Tessa's age. Things might have been different. With someone to smile at him, to express the tiniest bit of pride in him, instead of judgment and disappointment, he might not have tried so hard to prove the dire predictions correct. Maybe then…

"Isn't that right, Brother Andrew?"

The sound of his name ripped Andrew's thoughts back to the present, with only remnants of past pain coming along for the ride. "I'm sorry. What were you saying?"

"I was telling Mrs. Jacobs that we usually go to the Big Boy after church," Reverend Bob said.

"Sure thing. I never miss it, especially the chance for an ice cream sundae." Funny, he'd have given anything to miss it today. He needed to get his head together, to figure out why he felt this need to be near Serena.

"Mommy, can we have ice cream?" Tessa asked as she and Hannah skipped past on their way back out the front door.

Over her shoulder, Hannah yelled at them. "Yeah, Dad. Me, too."

Reverend Bob turned back to Serena. "Then, it's settled. You'll go with us."

Andrew didn't like the way his insides betrayed him by turning to gelatin. He stiffened, hoping to cover his internal weakness. "Sure, Serena, it'll be fun, and a great opportunity for your local pastoral staff to grill you about your past."

Serena rolled her eyes. "Sounds great."

Reverend Bob turned to the two women behind

Andrew. "You'll join us, too, won't you Laura and Charity?"

Andrew looked away to hide his grimace. Why did he not want the woman who'd pursued him relentlessly in the same room with the one he wanted to assist through a tough time? It shouldn't have made any difference. But it did. Charity would see Serena as a threat. Whether the threat was real or fictional wouldn't make any difference. And he was smart enough to realize Charity wouldn't be kind to the competition.

"Do you have a career outside the home, Mrs. Jacobs?" Reverend Bob asked, after wiping his mouth on a napkin.

Several smaller tables had been pushed together forming a table so long that Hannah and Laura, sitting on opposite ends, couldn't converse without yelling.

"Not *outside* the home, but I do have a job in addition to parenting." Serena set her fork aside. "I'm a freelance writer."

"What do you write?" Reverend Bob asked.

"Oh, everything from advertising copy to magazine articles to text for Web pages—about anything, as long as it pays and it's legal."

"What does *Mr. Jacobs* think about you spending so much time at home away from housework and your child?" Charity smiled sweetly as if she had not just asked an incredibly tacky question.

Serena swallowed hard, her mind searching

wildly for any reply that would somehow keep her dignity, while putting this unprovoked attacker in her place. As much as she wanted to say that Mr. Jacobs was too busy bothering the new Mrs. Jacobs to have any time to annoy her, she doubted it would have the desired effect.

"I'm a single-parent. Working at home is a financial necessity. It helps me make ends meet."

Charity nodded and took a drink of her water, making it clear that she'd gotten the message. The way Andrew, sandwiched between Charity and her mother, seemed to be fighting back a grin, told Serena he approved of her approach. Why that mattered, she wasn't sure. Serena counted the seconds until the can of worms exploded, and her wait was short.

"Are you a widow, then, dear? Or are you *divorced?*" Laura's distaste was clear in the acidic way she said the word.

"Divorced," Serena answered.

"That's unfortunate."

Unfortunate for whom—for my family because of the difficult challenge we're facing or for your family because you think I might be competition? Now, why had she thought that? It wasn't like her to be mean-spirited, but lately nothing about her resembled her former self.

Reverend Bob planted his hands on the side of the table, just as he planted them every Sunday on the edges of the lectern, and like magic, all attention turned to him. Instead of making some momentous announcement, he changed the subject. "Serena, I suspect you and Charity are about the same age. She is a nurse at West Oakland Regional Hospital, in Labor and Delivery."

Serena smiled at Charity, pitying any mother who had to deliver a baby under her watch. No, she had to give the woman the benefit of a doubt. Charity was probably just having a bad day. "That must be a great job, watching all of those babies come into the world."

Charity didn't smile. "Except when it's not… when there are problems in delivery. Or worse. On those days, I'd just as soon be somewhere else, working checkout at a discount store or something."

Her eyes were suddenly shiny, and she stared out the window at something only she could see. Serena's eyes burned at the thought of the devastating losses Charity would have witnessed. How had she handled it? Serena couldn't imagine the pain those parents must have faced. She didn't even want to.

Automatically, she turned to the end of the table where Tessa and Hannah were playing ticktacktoe on the back of a place mat, oblivious to everyone else at lunch. Reaching into her satchel, she withdrew a plastic bag containing Tessa's medication and a liquid measuring syringe. "Here, Tessa, take your medicine."

"No, I want Hannah to give it to me."

It wasn't worth the battle right now. "Hannah, will you do it?"

Hannah administered the medicine easily. Serena

put the supplies away and went back to her chicken sandwich.

Reverend Bob finally broke the silence that had settled around them. "Why does Tessa take medication?"

Serena filled them in on the major details of Tessa's illness, surprised that her words produced no more than a small ache. Maybe it would only get easier.

Laura watched Hannah and Tessa, who were shoving coins in the candy machines near the exit. "Oh, the poor dear. She's such a sweet little thing."

Serena warmed just watching her giggling child. "She's a real trooper."

She tried to stop her thoughts from traveling down their typical dark path of pain. Studying her hands for a few seconds, she looked up to see Andrew watching her, his expression compassionate. Without his moving, he seemed to reach over to touch her hand. She was surprised at how she was comforted by that thought. Who could blame her? It seemed like a lifetime since anyone had offered her support.

Andrew pushed back from the table and tucked his hands in his suit pockets. "Have I told everyone that Serena is the newest Sunday School teacher in the youth group? She starts next Sunday."

"How did that little assignment come about?" Charity sounded agitated, although her expression was unreadable.

"That's what I would like to know." Serena figured a little mood lightening couldn't hurt in this room.

Andrew shook his head, snickering. "It started out when Serena saved me from having to cancel the youth lock-in by volunteering to serve as one of the chaperones."

"How did you happen to ask Serena, since she's new to Hickory Ridge?" Laura's voice sounded pleasant enough, but her jaw looked strained.

"Are you kidding?" Andrew held both hands palms up. "I asked everyone I could think of first. Serena was my last—and I mean last—resort."

Serena did her best to look offended. "And I thought he needed my individual talent."

They all had a good laugh at that—even Tessa, who'd returned from the candy machines and was chomping on a wad of gum that she'd no doubt swallow within minutes. Only Charity and Laura refrained from joining in.

The gathering wound down quickly after that, with Laura insisting on covering the entire check. Andrew seemed oddly quiet, and Serena wondered if it was about the check or something else. It surprised her how unsettled she felt at his discomfort. And it was equally surprising how strongly she felt the need to make him happy again.

Andrew remained quiet during the car ride back to the church with Reverend Bob. Thankfully, Bob didn't try to start a conversation. When they pulled into the drive, Andrew was already gripping the door handle.

"Thanks for the ride, Bob."

"Wait, I wanted to talk to you for a minute."

Immediately Andrew regretted accepting the ride with the minister, especially since Reverend Bob's own daughter had caught a ride with Serena and Tessa. He just wanted to get inside the house and into his personal space, where he could dissect the events of the past few days. Every minute since Serena Jacobs walked into his office seemed to have passed in a blur.

"Sure. What did you need?"

"I wanted to talk with you about these new developments in the youth department." Reverend Bob shut off the engine, providing the clue that the conversation wouldn't be brief. "With Serena teaching the junior high children, the department will become so much more manageable."

"Yes, it will be nice to finally teach Sunday School for just the senior high level, instead of both."

Reverend Bob nodded. "Based on Hannah's reaction to her—and I trust my daughter's instincts—I'd say Serena will be a great addition to the department."

Andrew gazed cross the church grounds to the woods beyond, seeing Serena's face in the center of it all. "Yeah, she's great, isn't she. The kids flock to her like she's handing out candy bars or something. There's a very real quality to her—probably all of the things she's overcome—that the kids respond to.''

"Hannah certainly does," Reverend Bob said. "Already she has connected with both Serena and Tessa. I'm glad to see it. They may be really good for Hannah. She's avoided getting close to people, except a few school friends, since Deborah died. Serena might just be the key to getting through to her—to helping *me* reach her.''

"You may be right.''

"At least she'll be a woman Hannah can talk to.''

"Serena will do more than that. I just know it.'' Look at the way she'd already made his life a whole lot easier—professionally, of course. She affected others without even trying. "She has so much to offer. Her compassion, her charm—even a sense of humor that she doesn't use as much as she should. Then there's her faith, which she's barely begun to cultivate.''

All the words had spilled from his mouth before he could stop them. He'd said too much, and he knew it. He turned toward Reverend Bob, dreading his reaction. The minister tapped out a nervous percussion solo on his steering wheel, watching him.

Andrew shifted in his seat and grasped for an escape. "Have I shown you the summer youth activity schedule? It's jam-packed. These kids will be too busy to blow their noses, let alone get into trouble.''

"That's good in theory, but over the years I've learned that if they want to get into trouble, they'll find the time.'' Reverend Bob slowed his tapping and faced Andrew again. "That was an interesting lunch."

"Interesting is one way to describe it."

"Charity Sims seems to have a personal interest in you."

Andrew turned back toward him. "You're only noticing that now?"

"No, I've observed several signs over the past few months. What I haven't seen is any sign that you return her feelings."

"That's right. I've tried to hint that her idea isn't going to work out, but she never seems to listen to subtle messages."

Reverend Bob nodded. "Be careful of the less-than-subtle ones. I know you wouldn't want to hurt her feelings."

"Of course not, but she's making it very difficult."

"I see."

Andrew took a good look at his minister, wondering what Reverend Bob really did see. And what did he think about whatever assumptions he had wrongly—or rightly—made? As casually as he could, Andrew broke off the conversation and got out of the car.

He watched the taillights as the blue sedan turned out of the drive, then released the breath he'd been holding. Still, he couldn't relax. Even Reverend Bob had seen it. His true feelings were as transparent as a plate-glass window—and just as prone to being shattered.

Chapter Five

Andrew parked his Chevrolet Prizm in front of Serena's house, with second, third and fourth thoughts already plaguing him. Maybe this wasn't a good idea after all. But if it wasn't, he sure hoped he hadn't gone to a lot of trouble—for nothing—gathering all of these teens on his day off.

He peered in the rear-view mirror at the teenagers crammed into the back. A church van would be a smart purchase, but with the groundbreaking on the construction project planned next summer, the deacons could barely afford *his* salary.

"It's getting hot in here," said one voice that rose from the mass of bodies in the back seat.

"Who skipped deodorant this morning?" another asked.

Andrew shrugged. The worst Serena could say was no. He ignored the uncomfortable feeling that possibility gave him. "Okay, everybody out."

He got out and opened the rear driver's-side door, while Hannah, who was riding shotgun, did the same on the passenger side. Within seconds, three more almost-full-size humans emerged and followed Andrew to the door. He took a deep breath and knocked.

Tessa swung open the front door, as Serena emerged from the kitchen behind her, wiping her hands on a dishtowel.

"What did I say about not opening the door to strangers, Tessa?"

"It's not a stranger. It's Mr. Andrew, Mommy."

Andrew waited until Serena reached the doorway before he spoke. "She does have a point."

"He brought big kids...and Hannah." Tessa spoke the older girl's name with awe.

Hannah stepped to the front of the crowd, crouching to face Tessa through the screen door. "Andrew's taking all of us to the beach at Kensington Metropark. We want you guys to come with us."

Serena frowned. "Oh, I wish you had called us first."

So you could have gotten out of it easier? No way. But Andrew only smiled. "I'm sorry, but it was an impromptu thing. I'll try to remember that next time you like to have...warning." He dragged out the words, hoping his little helper would do her job.

"Mommy, can we go to the beach? *Please?*" Tessa tugged on Serena's arm.

One of these days he'd have to thank Tessa for that.

Serena glanced at Tessa, at Andrew and around at the four teenage faces. Her frustrated expression told him just when she realized she'd lost.

"Well, I suppose we can go for a little while. But we have to make it back in time for your nap."

"You wouldn't mind driving a few kids, would you? I don't have enough seat belts in my car to legally transport them, so I haven't picked up the last two." Andrew tried to ignore the absolute glee that filled him, which didn't even seem to be over winning the point. Whatever the feeling was about, he couldn't afford to think about it now—not with her standing this close.

As if she were reading his thoughts, Serena raised an eyebrow and dragged her teeth across her bottom lip. "I don't mind. Just let us grab our suits and towels."

A trickle of sweat formed at Andrew's nape and slid down his spine. He was wearing a swimsuit himself. Why hadn't he gauged the likelihood that Serena would also wear one? Just the mental image of her in a swimsuit was enough to make him question the logic of planning this "impromptu" beach outing. How could he maintain his dignity without becoming a bumbling fool when they were at the beach together, soaking up sunshine?

Serena inhaled the fresh lake air—the scent of cut grass tinged with dew—closing her eyes and tilting her head skyward to feel the sun's heat on her face. She hoped her casual facade would mask her nervousness as she peeled off her oversize T-shirt and settled back on her beach towel in her standby black maillot.

Would he be disappointed by the way she looked in a swimsuit? Would he even notice? She tried to shake away the adolescent thoughts that shamed her. She didn't want him to look, and at the same time, she was scared he wouldn't.

"This is great. I'm glad you forced us to come," Serena said, giving him a sidelong glance.

The look in his eyes when Andrew pulled off his sunglasses was pure innocence. She'd relaxed for the first time, once she felt sand between her toes. But his gaze held hers too long, and her tenuous calm evaporated faster than the sunscreen she'd rubbed on her nose.

"What do you mean 'forced'?"

When he swallowed hard, she was almost glad to recognize he felt even an ounce of her nervousness. "Don't play innocent with me. It was a good touch bringing all the kids along and asking in front of Tessa. If their presence hadn't convinced me, you were sure that telling me two other kids were still stuck at home would, right?"

He slipped on his sunglasses and settled back on the blanket. "What can I say? I needed another chaperone."

Serena chuckled and tried not to notice how handsome Andrew looked in his vibrant blue swim trunks, lying back on his towel with his eyes closed. A cross on a long gold chain lay off-center on his chest. She wondered if there was a story that went with that cross. Maybe it was a gift from his parents or an old girlfriend. But why did she hope it was the former?

When he wasn't watching her, when she didn't have a sense of being trapped—and warmed—by his stare, she was amazed at how good she felt being near him. Safe. When was the last time she'd felt this way?

She sat up and looked out at the water, where the teens were playing some game in which Tessa climbed from one set of shoulders to the next, with only her feet up to her ankles ever touching the water.

Hannah, with Tessa on her shoulders, made a dash for a lean, blond boy that Serena couldn't remember having seen before at church. Tessa moved smoothly from Hannah's shoulders to the boy's.

"Who's that new guy?"

Andrew lifted up on his elbows and looked across the water. "His name is Todd McBride. He's Hannah's neighbor. He's visited church a few times. I guess he helped her a lot when her mom died two years ago."

"I knew Reverend Bob was a widower, but I didn't realize it had happened so recently."

Andrew shook his head. "I don't think either of them is close to being over it."

He had such a faraway look that Serena wondered whether he was still talking about his boss's tragedy or something more personal. When he leaned forward and rubbed his leg, she watched his hands until they stopped on a narrow, white scar. She tried not to stare, but it had to be about seven inches long, starting midway on his calf and stretching over his ankle. How had she not noticed that before? She would have asked about it if he hadn't caught her staring and answered her unspoken question.

"It's from a motorcycle accident when I was about nineteen."

He pressed his lips together, signaling that the subject was closed, but she guessed there was a lot more to it. For a reason she couldn't explain, she just had to know.

"Motorcycle? Didn't I see a Harley-Davidson poster in your room?"

He nodded and stared at the water, seeming intent on studying the ripples across the dark surface. "Yes, and if you were to look in the old barn behind the house, you would find the real thing. An '83 Harley Low Rider. I learned a tough lesson with it, but I still keep it around."

"What lesson?"

"That you don't rev a Hog's engine and race through downtown on it when you're plastered. It can mean an arrest record for you, as well as pain and physical therapy for you *and* your victim."

He'd admitted to having been a drunk driver, an action she'd always thought of as unforgivable. But all she could focus on was his expression, which spoke of unresolved agony and self-judgment. He hated himself far more than anyone else could for his mistakes. Any criticism from her seemed out of place.

Her arms ached to pull him close. She wanted to rock him the way she did Tessa when the child's pain became unbearable. That reaction was purely maternal, she told herself. She was simply responding as she would to any boy or girl in need.

But Andrew Westin wasn't a boy. He was a man. That he was in a tortured state of mind only made her choice of words more critical. "It sounds as if you've learned an awful lot."

"If you mean that I don't drink and drive—or that I don't drink at all, for that matter—then, you're right. But I still love to ride. There's just something about having the wind in your face, the power under your seat and the scenery whipping by." He leaned on his elbows, the tension of moments before absent. "It's a great escape."

"What are you trying to escape from?"

Instead of answering, Andrew leaped up and sprinted toward the water. Whatever it was, he was still running. She should let him have his secret, but his reticence made her even more curious. She watched him run a few beats longer and then, not one to skip a challenge, raced after him.

She stamped into the water—which was colder than she would have expected—as he came up from a dive. If he thought this conversation was over, he was underestimating her memory. What was he running from? It surprised her how much she longed to help him face his ghosts.

Serena waded farther into the water, trying not to notice the lake plants grabbing her feet. She should have laughed at the irony of this switch from the "helped" to the "helper." But a hard tug on her ankle sent her face first into the water. She came up sputtering. Counting the teens and their pint-size partner, all doubled over in laughter, she guessed her attacker by process of elimination.

"Westin, you're a dead man."

She swam after him, knowing the water in the roped-off swim area was so shallow that she'd have done as well to jog. Before long, she couldn't breathe, and she hurt all over. It was frustrating being this out of shape. That Andrew also was gasping for breath when she caught up with him was comforting, but it didn't make her forget her mission. She dunked him from behind before he even caught his breath.

He surfaced with her hands still gripping his arms. When he flexed his biceps, she realized what a mistake it had been to touch him. Her fingers tingled at the point of contact. As much as she wanted to let go, she couldn't help but touch for a few seconds longer. Too long to go unnoticed.

She released him, planning to swim away and escape the moment's intensity, but he stood and turned to face her. His stare held her as firmly as if the sand under her feet had been mixed with quick-set concrete.

Just what was he hoping to see, looking at her that way? Whatever it was, it made him smile, and that expression delivered its own electric charge. Allowing the current to flow between them was ill-advised, given that they were standing in water. Well, electrocution would have been no more shocking than her realization that she could be attracted to a man again, despite her own emotional scars.

"You trying to get away before I dunk you again?" Andrew's tone was light despite the weighted air.

She bent over and took a deep, steadying breath. "I couldn't swim another lap if my life depended upon it. My legs feel like rubber and my lungs are on fire."

He let go of a huge breath. "Good, I'd hoped I wasn't the only one who would have to admit I was getting old."

Serena reached out into a sidestroke. "I admit nothing of the kind."

Andrew slid through the water on his side, as well. "Let's call it a truce before we both have a coronary."

That truce lasted until the first few points of the no-net volleyball game. On opposite sides and matched with the kids—with Tessa keeping score—they set and spiked to an eventual tie. Serena collapsed on her towel, exhausted. Resting on her elbows, she watched Tessa and Hannah playing architect on some sand castle mega-mall, with Todd filling in as construction crew. Some of the kids splashed in the water while others tossed a sponge football on the sand.

Todd grabbed Tessa and twirled her in the air. "Let's bury her in the sand."

"Yeah, she'll make a great sand sculpture." Hannah scooted over to tickle Tessa's toes.

Giggles filled the afternoon air as Tessa lay on the sand and slowly evolved into a mound with toes and a face.

Serena didn't have a watch, but from the sun, she could tell that it was well past nap time. She hated to ruin Tessa's fun, but it would be a mistake to let the child miss her afternoon snooze. Serena worried, and worrying made her mad. It wasn't fair that she couldn't let her little girl have a wonderful afternoon without having to analyze the impact of her decision. This was just one day. She'd already slathered sunscreen on Tessa several times to counteract the effect of her medication, which made her burn easily. That had to be enough. Tessa needed some normalcy. They both deserved that much.

"She's doing really well lately, isn't she."

At his voice, Serena realized that Andrew had plopped back down beside her. Was it to protect herself that she stiffened and sat up, pulling her T-shirt over her head? Funny, this guy laid her soul bare every time she spoke to him, and the best she could do was cover up her naked shoulders.

"Yes, she is, and all I can do is wait for the bottom to drop out. Doesn't that seem ridiculous?"

"Just understandable." He patted her shoulder, quickly removing his hand. Suddenly, he seemed overly interested in the sand castle Tessa had started with her friends after emerging from her sculpture. "What do you think of that castle? We could have used the Jacobs-Woods-McBride architectural agency for the Family Life Center."

Serena examined the moat Tessa was widening by scooping handfuls of sand. "Good idea. If I send Tessa to work, then I can quit freelancing."

She lowered her sunglasses so she could watch the development of the construction project, with its foam-cup-shaped towers and stick-lined bridges. Tessa wiggled between the two older kids, causing structural damage, but Todd and Hannah just used a little water and pasted the debris back into form.

The laughter that filled the air worked its way right inside Serena's heart. She wished Tessa could be this happy every day. As she watched the trio, something else caught her attention. Todd seemed to be peeking at Hannah with amazing regularity. It wasn't so much the fact he looked at her, as the *way* he did so. Weren't they supposed to be just friends? But his observation of Hannah—her smiles, her laughs, the way she tucked her hair behind her ear— hinted otherwise.

Serena glanced at Andrew to see if he was watching the same thing. A flutter of recognition awakened in her belly before she fully processed what she'd seen. Andrew wasn't watching any interaction between Todd and Hannah, or anyone else for that matter. He was too busy staring at her.

The brochure on Serena's computer screen sat there, looking as uninspired as it had since they'd returned home two hours earlier. If she submitted this project in its current form to her client, she could forget future work or any referrals. She rubbed her hands across her exhausted face, feeling the fever of sunburn on her cheeks.

Maybe the sun had baked her brain, as well. It certainly had knocked Tessa out. She'd been asleep ever since the car ride, not even budging when Serena had accidentally bumped the child's head on the wall on the way up the stairs. Even if she was tired now, Tessa had had a wonderful day.

Serena tried hard to focus on the joy she'd witnessed in her daughter's face today, but her mind kept drifting to another face with feelings that were equally readable. The same warring emotions flowed through her now as had done so at the moment she'd caught Andrew staring. Fierce flattery. Pure panic. She'd had to fight herself not to stare right back. Thankfully, he'd looked away first.

Whether the look they'd shared was over or not made no difference. It was imprinted far below the surface of her skin. And it made her tremble from her eyebrows to the arches of her feet.

Exasperated, Serena closed her computer file, leaped up and shoved her office chair to the desk. She wasn't getting any work done, anyway. So she left her business assignment, hoping she was also leaving behind her unacceptable thoughts.

The images followed her, though, dogging her while she flitted from laundry basket to dishwasher to the relentless stack of bills. An overreaction. That had to be what this was. Andrew had been nice to her. He'd shown concern for her and Tessa over this difficult time in their lives. She was simply making too much out of it.

With that settled, she headed into the kitchen to prepare dinner. It was good to put all her restless energy to some practical use—chopping vegetables, browning meat and combining just the right spices.

When she finally finished puttering around the kitchen, she had a full pot of spaghetti sauce simmering on the stove. What was she going to do with it all? There was no way that she and Tessa would be able to eat all of this, even if Tessa's steroids made her ravenous enough to eat seconds or thirds.

What she needed was a friend to share the meal with, someone with a hearty appetite. Maybe even a bachelor who could use a home-cooked meal. It would help them both. With dinner, she could pay back Andrew for helping her to return to the real world. He could have some home cooking, and she'd have adult company. This would even be a good opportunity for him to bring her Sunday School teaching manual and discuss Bible study goals.

All of her justifications sounded perfectly reasonable and defendable. She could almost convince herself they were true.

But her tremor of excitement as she lifted the phone made the lie she was telling herself very clear.

Chapter Six

Andrew felt more nervous than an adolescent on his way to the prom when he walked up the steps to Serena's house, a two-liter bottle of soda pop stowed under his arm. At least they were good enough friends that he wouldn't be expected to grip her hand with his soggy palm. Of course, tonight's dinner wasn't a date. It just felt like one, and he liked that feeling more than he cared to admit.

He need not have worried about shaking hands when he knocked at the door. "Hey Serena. It's Andrew."

"Come on in," she called. "I'm in the kitchen."

The tiny room was easy to find. He had only to follow his nose to the smells of oregano, basil and garlic. His mouth watered during the dozen or so steps to the kitchen.

Since this was the first time he'd made it past her living room to the rear of the house, he took a few seconds to scan the gold-speckled tile and the out-dated harvest-gold appliances. Serena had told him this place was a rental from a friend of a friend.

Her little touches—cream eyelet tie-back curtains and the matching tablecloth on the dinette—had done a lot to update the disco-era look. Everything she'd done to fix up their home—from the kitchen and living room to Tessa's sunny bedroom—seemed focused on making the place the brightest it could be for her little girl.

That was it. Something had been missing when he had walked through the front door. There was no extra weight he'd come to expect at his knee. "Where's Tessa?"

Was it hurt that momentarily flashed across Serena's eyes before she smiled?

"She's still napping. Poor kid. Today really wore her out. We need to get her up soon, but maybe we should wait until…dinner's ready."

As if suddenly struck mute, she pressed her lips together and tucked a stray strand of hair behind her ear. His breath caught in his throat. How could he not have noticed earlier? Although she was wearing a green apron for her culinary work, it was apparent she'd taken some extra care with her appearance. Her dark hair had been brushed until it shone with the new highlights from an afternoon of sun. She was even wearing makeup.

Didn't she know she was just as beautiful with her hair tied in a sloppy knot, as it had been at the beach, without the assistance of artificial glamour on her skin? Still, he was secretly pleased that she'd fussed for him. She'd even donned a sleeveless fuchsia dress that showed off her new tan.

"Hey, you look great. The sun likes you."

She shook her head, a blush creeping up her neck. "I hope it doesn't decide it hates me when I get older."

Funny, Andrew couldn't imagine her as anything but lovely, no matter how many wrinkles or age spots appeared through the years. She turned suddenly to the sink and washed her hands. How long had he been staring? At least long enough to have sent her running. Now the best he could do was to pretend everything was normal, while they both knew it wasn't.

"Is there anything I can do in here?"

"Over there—" She handed him a knife and directed him farther down the counter to the cutting board covered with vegetables. A few minutes later, he'd already built an incredible vegetable salad, if he did say so himself, when he smelled something burning.

They were still making "burned bread" jokes a half-hour later when he returned with the replacement garlic loaf. They couldn't stop chuckling as they sat at the dinette. Only Tessa wasn't laughing. She looked tired and was surly.

Andrew took a big bite of his bread and frowned at Tessa. "This bread is missing something. I know. It's that delightfully charred taste. Do you know where I can get some with that taste?"

Tessa just frowned and rubbed her eyes.

Serena stuck out her tongue and laughed again. "You know, I might be able to set you up. I hope you don't mind, though. That old loaf now has extra flavoring from carrot peels, green pepper seeds and coffee grounds. Still want some?"

"Absolutely."

"Ew, that sounds yucky," Tessa chimed, finally aiming a drippy bite of spaghetti toward her mouth.

That was the last nice comment Tessa made during dinner, which turned from pleasant to stressful. It was difficult to make cheerful conversation when Tessa was whining about everything from the spaghetti being too hot, to her chair being pushed too close to the table. Even being told to finish her milk brought her to tears.

Serena allowed Tessa to have the fruit salad dessert, even though she hadn't eaten her dinner, and then she convinced Tessa to lie on the couch and watch her *Veggie Tales* video. Madame Blueberry had barely crooned about being blue, before Tessa was asleep.

Andrew watched the child, so sweet in sleep. How could her mother bear to see her hurting? Serena's life had to be just as difficult, and she was facing her difficult road alone. He wanted to make her life easier in some small way, so when she carried her daughter to bed, he rushed to clear the dishes and put on coffee. He had steaming mugs on the table when she returned.

"Thanks. I should never have let her miss her

nap.'' Serena sat and wrapped her hands around her mug, perhaps too tightly.

Andrew stopped lifting his cup before it reached his lips and lowered it again. He felt her discomfort so intensely that he wondered if it hadn't started with him after all. He defended them both. "She was having a great time. You saw that. It was good for her to have a normal day that wasn't all about JRA."

Serena absently stirred her coffee, although she was drinking it black. "I know you're right, but she's just so overtired. That can't be good for her. The guides for parents of kids with arthritis suggest that even older kids rest after school because their condition makes them tire so easily."

"She'll nap like normal tomorrow, and she'll be fine."

She didn't believe him, and he knew it. He rose and went to the sink, and she followed; together they washed and dried dishes in companionable silence. It felt good being near her, even performing that routine task. Until that moment, he hadn't realized how lonely he'd been.

Andrew peered at her profile as she dried the last glass. Serena looked so frail tonight. Most days— even the day she'd asked for help in conquering her depression—she seemed invincible. Asking for help when she needed it was just another sign of her strength.

But tonight she'd been laid bare. A different part of him responded to this new vulnerability. He wanted to know everything about her, to protect her from all enemies, real or imaginary.

"Everything's going to be okay. You know that, don't you, Serena?"

"Is it?"

She was asking about far more than a day of missed rest, and he could guarantee that no more than he could guarantee another day of awakening to morning. But he nodded, anyway. She needed him to be sure, even when she wasn't.

He searched for a way to ask her for some of the answers he craved, for insights into her soul. His opportunity passed when she poured them more coffee and headed with hers into the living room. He followed and found her looking out the screen door to the curb.

"Tell me about the motorcycle."

He stared at the Hog parked out front, seeing ally and enemy wrapped in chrome. He wanted to cry 'foul' at her attempt to redirect the conversation from herself, but he was too caught up in the past. "What do you want to know?"

"The story behind it."

"I told you about the drunk driving charge."

She turned to him. "That's the result. I want to know about the beginning."

He felt as if he were slowly opening a can of worms that was better left under the airtight seal of his memory. "I was a rebellious kid."

She smiled, sitting on the couch and motioning

for him to sit at the other end. "I'd guessed that."
She said nothing else but her silence requested more.

He wanted to stop, to leave well enough alone, although it would never be *well enough* or even *okay*. The words came despite his best effort at containing them. "I was trying to hurt my parents, I guess, but I ended up hurting myself—and other innocent people—more."

Her eyes widened with the innocence of one who'd known only love and acceptance in her childhood. For a few seconds, he wished...why did he still want something he'd never had?

"Why did you want to hurt them?"

"Not everyone had a loving family like you did. Mine was all about expectations, about impossible goals. They demanded perfection and were shocked and mean when I didn't measure up. Even the name they chose for me was about expectations. Andrew—one of the Twelve Apostles. Jesus's handpicked followers. From the very beginning, I was set up to fail."

He tightened his jaw and fought back the words that painted his memory like an abandoned building's wall of graffiti. *You're sinful, boy. God's penalty for sin is death, so feel glad that you're tasting only our punishment so far.*

She faced him, leaning forward and resting her elbows on her knees. Her eyes shone with pity that he neither wanted nor deserved.

"Did they...hurt you?"

"Not in the way you're thinking. They probably

thought they were doing God's will by never sparing the rod or softening the sting of their constant criticism." He needed to shut up. The words hurt too much. But he felt the need to be heard and understood. Just this once. "We were in church every time the doors were unlocked. But nothing they heard from the pulpit convinced them to treat me with love once we got home."

"If they were people of faith, how could they hurt their child that way?"

He shook his head, pondering that same question for the millionth time. "I was a product of their religious training and a constant disappointment. But the God they introduced me to was nothing like the Lord you and I know. He was all about damnation instead of deliverance, about fire and brimstone instead of enduring love."

"No wonder you rebelled."

Andrew searched Serena's face for more of the condemnation he'd come to expect. What he saw was acceptance—something that had come from so few people in his life. Did she see something in him that his parents had missed?

At that moment, Serena seemed more dangerous than she had at any time since he'd first recognized his attraction for her. If she believed in him now, and if he allowed himself to rely on that belief, then it was only a matter of time until he would disappoint her. For a reason he couldn't explain, he was positive that failing Serena would be more than he could bear.

He needed an out in this conversation, and he found one when he peered through the window at his motorcycle. "I guess that was a roundabout way of telling you about the Harley. Riding it makes me feel free, but it's more than that. It represents that rebellion—about the drinking, womanizing and attempted self-destruction—that nearly led to tragedy. Things I should never forget."

She cocked her head. "Doesn't it also represent how far you've come?"

He'd never thought of it that way. It was true he'd made progress, but he still had a long way to go to prove himself. If that were even possible. "I don't know. Maybe. But I think, most important, it reminds me of my focus as youth minister. I want to help kids make friends with the God I know now, rather than the image of Him that was shoved down my throat."

Serena settled back into the couch, setting her coffee aside and kicking off her sandals. "I knew you'd have some interesting stories to tell. That scar—" she glanced at the permanent stamp of his irresponsibility "—was just one of the hints."

Her words, and the close of the subject that came with them, felt like a gift. The conversation had become a vise around his neck, and he was grateful for a chance to breathe. But he had to prevent her from starting again.

"We all have our stories, Serena. Tell me about your divorce."

The way her posture transformed, from curved to

straight, spoke volumes about the suffering she'd refused to admit. Her reaction caused the muscles in his stomach to clench. He couldn't acknowledge the response as jealousy because that meant he felt something he couldn't afford to feel.

Silence lingered as Serena stared at the wall, probably reliving buried experiences he'd had no right to exhume. He needed to apologize, had to find the right words. She saved him the trouble by answering.

"I told you he cheated on me."

"It can't be as simple as that."

Serena shivered inside at the memory that still stung like a new wound. She licked her lips and scanned the room—anything to delay the words a few seconds more. "I guess not. I'd suspected it several times before. But the last time was different."

She waited for him to say something, to prod her somehow, but he only nodded. It calmed her that he'd slipped back into his counselor role. But Andrew was more than an impartial listener to her now. He was a friend. That comforted her even more. Still, nothing made the story any easier or any less humiliating to tell.

"He'd been distant ever since Tessa first got sick. Often when she had appointments for testing, he'd be too busy at work to get away." The same irritation that had boiled inside her at the time began to bubble again. "Then he started having to stay late at the office."

Andrew shifted in his seat until his leg curled up on the cushion. "So you weren't surprised when it happened?"

"Overall I wasn't, but the *way* it happened shocked me to death." As she closed her eyes, the pain of those memories became a tangible thing that she could touch in her mind, but she couldn't bat it away with her hands. She breathed deeply and pressed past the hurt, searching for relief that wouldn't come. "The day we had Tessa's bone marrow extraction to rule out leukemia, he didn't show up at the hospital. I kept calling his office, but he was signed out for the day."

"Was he with someone else?" His words sounded calm but his jaw was tight.

She let Andrew's words swirl through her thoughts for a few seconds. Such a simple question about something with such devastating consequences. If she continued to hold these thoughts at arm's length, perhaps she could protect herself from feeling anything. A voice inside her, though, called out with its own opinion: *silly girl.*

If she'd had any inkling she was going to cry, Serena could have been prepared. One second she felt the burning behind her eyes, and the next, her lips tasted salty. Tiny wet spots dotted the front of her dress. Brushing at them, she glanced at Andrew, hoping he had looked away. He hadn't.

He scooted close to her and took both of her hands in his. His comfort felt personal, more so than the carefully distant compassion of a professional counselor. He really cared. And she needed someone to care right now. It was so easy to feel protected with her hands clasped in the firm but gentle pressure of his.

For her self-preservation, she should stop talking about this. She'd already said too much, given rebirth to long-dead emotions. But she couldn't seem to stop. She needed Andrew to understand the violation she'd felt.

"When he should have been there, comforting his child, he was spending the day with a co-worker, forgetting his marriage vows and seeking comfort for himself."

She was grateful that the mental numbness from that day returned now. The only sensation she felt was the tightening grip of Andrew's hands. Even without the squeeze, she would have recognized his anger from his stiff posture and the pulse ticking at his temple. His anger on her behalf was as comforting as a warm hug.

"How did you find out?" His words were clipped, as though he'd forced them through clenched teeth.

"That was easy. I had come home with Tessa that afternoon. She was still crabby from the anesthesia. I was trying to calm her down while hiding my own fury with Trent. It had had all day to build."

Gently, she pulled her hands from Andrew's grasp. She needed to get through her next words without support.

"When he walked through the door, I laid into

him over his failings. I'd barely gotten started when he turned to me angrily. He told me he'd spent the day in Dawn's arms.'' Funny, she expected more tears then, but her eyes were dry. Maybe she'd finally cried them out. ''He asked for a divorce so he could be with her.''

Andrew's hands tightened so hard into fists that his knuckles flashed white. He jumped up from the couch and paced the living room's limited space.

His words were softly spoken but not quiet enough for her to miss. ''He was an idiot to ever leave you.''

A sudden chill whipped through her. It wasn't so much what he'd said as the passion with which he'd said it. From his shocked expression, she could see he knew he'd revealed too much.

Silence clung like the humid air outside. Realization spoke louder than words ever could. Serena searched for some way to ease the awkwardness. Things between them would never be the same—not now. She continued as if his words hadn't just changed everything.

''We'd been having trouble for a long time…beyond my suspicions of his infidelity. The problems didn't become grossly apparent until Tessa got sick.'' She waited for Andrew to return to the couch before continuing. ''Trent just couldn't handle the fact that our daughter wasn't perfect. It was hard enough for me to handle. But Tessa was still there, needing meals, baths and bedtime stories.''

He leaned back into the cushions. "You buckled down and did what you had to do."

Serena shook her head. "It wasn't as simple as that. I didn't have the luxury of distancing myself from the pain the way Trent did, and I resented it. I'm sure I was critical all the time."

"But it was his choice to be unfaithful," Andrew shot back. "Just as it was your choice to be there for your daughter."

"'Choice'? It's funny that you would use that word." Serena sunk into the couch, depleted. "What choice did I have?"

He leaned forward and clasped his hands together before meeting her gaze. "You had the choice of standing up and accepting the life you were given or letting it destroy you. From what I can see, you triumphed, giving Tessa the strong support she needs and the best example of the woman she can become."

Couldn't he see she was none of the things he described? She was no Florence Nightingale-type heroine. She was just a mom, doing what she had to do for her child. A powerless and terrified mom. She focused on the wall's forest scene print. It was safer than the intensity of his stare. It didn't make her feel so vulnerable…so exposed. "I don't see that at all. All I see is a woman who keeps a good public face and then cries when nobody hears."

"I see it, Serena."

He placed his hands on her shoulders, their faces mere inches apart. This time his grip felt more like a caress than a touch of compassion. She suppressed a shiver that started inside but must have been detectable on the outside.

He was going to kiss her. Her mind whirled. She should discourage it, should do something to stop him. But her heart got in the way with its wishing and hoping. Looking up from the ground, Serena met his gaze. His expression was asking her for permission. Her own must have granted it, because he leaned closer still, so near that she could feel his warm breath touch her lips and could inhale the earthy scent of his hair.

Her eyes must have closed in preparation because they flew open at the cry that came from Tessa's room.

"Mommy!"

Guilt flooded through her as she jumped up from the couch and ran toward the stairs. How could she have been so selfish? She'd lost sight of what was important, allowed her own needs to take precedence over her child's. Tessa had to be her focus—and look how easily she'd forgotten that.

She flipped on the light as she passed through the doorway, her gaze glued to the tiny figure sobbing on the bed. She'd failed Tessa again.

Chapter Seven

"**I**'m here, sweetheart." Serena brushed Tessa's hair back from her face, feeling the telltale heat beneath her fingers. She pulled her daughter from beneath the sweat-soaked sheet and cradled her as she always did when the fevers came. She stepped backward and lowered herself into the rocking chair.

"Is she all right?" Andrew asked from the doorway.

Serena jerked at the sound. She hadn't remembered he was even there, let alone noticed he'd followed her up the stairs. She regarded him cautiously, already in mother-bear mode, and saw only a distraction from her purpose.

"It's just another fever. Maybe you'd better…"

Instead of taking her hint and retreating, he knelt by the chair, touching Tessa's brow. He jerked his hand back as if he'd been scorched. "Oh man, she's so hot."

"This is how it happens. All of a sudden, the fever spikes."

She directed him to the medicine cabinet to retrieve the thermometer and the non-aspirin fever reducer. The ear thermometer beeped at one hundred and four. Serena filled the liquid syringe and gave Tessa a dose.

Andrew paced the room, finally sitting on Tessa's bed. Why was he still there? She'd given him the perfect opportunity to escape guilt-free. Yet, he'd stayed.

"Shouldn't we take her to the emergency room?"

The word *we* rang in her ears, melding with the buzz of barely contained panic. She should have been used to these nights of frustration and helplessness by now, but she was still like a white-knuckle flyer during landing.

"No, she's had temperatures like this dozens of times, although her fevers are becoming less frequent and usually not as high...."

He leaned forward and brushed Tessa's hand. The child jerked in her light dozing. "Poor little girl. She's had an awful lot to put up with."

Serena hugged her child more tightly to her. She rocked, as much for herself as for Tessa.

It was a long time before Serena glanced across the dark room at the shadowed form sitting on the bed. Why hadn't Andrew run the way Trent always had? Obviously, he was just being kind, waiting for her to give him an exit.

"You'd better go home. Do you think you can let yourself out?" She leaned to kiss Tessa's brow.

"No, I can't."

She looked up, surprised. Why was he making this difficult? "There's nothing you can do tonight, so I'll call you tomorrow. I'm sure she'll be fine by morning."

Andrew didn't move and gave no indication he would. Silence stretched tension into a thin line. Only Tessa's occasional whimpers broke the taut constancy.

Serena stood and paced toward the window with Tessa in her arms. She stared into the darkness before turning back to see him. She'd been crazy to nearly allow him to kiss her. Now there were issues to explain—things that had to wait for a better time. When a good time would be, she couldn't imagine. But none could be worse than now. When he finally spoke, she jerked at the sound.

"I'm not going anywhere…until I know that Tessa is okay." He crossed his arms.

She opened her mouth to argue, but took one look at how straight he sat and thought better of it. He wouldn't negotiate on this. He was staying.

The realization shook her harder than the impact of his touch ever could have. But that was easier to accept than the warmth that spread through her insides. He'd been talking only about sticking around for one evening. It was a huge leap for her to see him as the kind of man who would stick beside her no matter how dark the day. And yet she was convinced of it. A few days ago, that thought would have sent her running, but tonight she craved peace too much to question it.

Andrew sat in the rocker, extending his arms toward her in a silent request to hold Tessa. Could she take a chance and place her child in another man's hands when already Tessa had experienced the pain of broken promises? The risk was too great. But he waited there, pulling at her reluctance, until she took the four largest steps in the universe and lowered Tessa into his arms.

At once her own arms felt empty, but her child turned and buried her face in Andrew's chest. If great wisdom could come out of babes' mouths, then their instinct to trust also could be an example.

He rocked slowly, pulling his fingers through Tessa's damp hair. Man and child, moving in unison, connected in spirit. No matter what happened in the future, this moment would forever be imprinted on Serena's heart. And no matter where she was, she'd still be glad that God had led Andrew Westin into their lives.

The next morning, Andrew tried to focus on the Bible study guide on his desk but between yawns, could only watch the words float on the page. Tessa's fever had taken forever to drop to just over one hundred degrees, but he'd been too stubborn to let her out of his arms. He just hadn't been able to, until he knew she was all right. How did Serena handle the uncertainty that JRA represented every day?

He was paying for last night's decisions in two ways: in exhaustion and in the realization that he'd allowed that little girl and her mother to break through the concrete barrier around his heart. He was on dangerous ground, pitted with land mines and snake lairs. How could he backpedal now?

"You're in a mess, old boy," he said to the walls of his office. As surprised as he was that he'd almost kissed Serena, he couldn't blame it on a strange combination of circumstances. He still wanted to kiss her, no matter how reckless it was to let her get that close to him.

Only Tessa's scream had stopped him. Otherwise, he would be in even deeper trouble than he already was. Had it happened because he finally understood how badly she'd been hurt and wanted to comfort her? He shook his head. It wasn't that simple.

"Lord, please give me the strength to do the right thing," he whispered, not having any idea what that right thing might be.

He tried to focus on the study guide. Still, he was thankful for the break when a knock came at his office door. Until Charity popped her head inside.

"Where were you all day yesterday?" She plopped in the chair opposite his desk. How like her it was to leap in with two feet instead of attempting small talk before a segue to more invasive stuff. "I kept trying to call you."

He tapped down the ire that was rising in him like

nasty bile. Why did she think she had the right to make him account for every minute of his life? Perhaps for the same reason some church members believed there were no boundaries between his public ministry and his personal life. That was one element of his job he was having trouble adjusting to.

"Monday is my day off. I took a group of the youth to the beach." He didn't see any reason to mention that Serena and Tessa were along for the trip.

"And you were catching rays until after eleven-thirty last night? That's the last time I called."

"Oh, sorry, I got home late. I hope it wasn't something critical."

At least she had the decency to look guilty. There was hope for her yet.

She chuckled. "Oh, no. Nothing like that. It was more like a birthday."

"Whose birthday?"

"Mother's."

"Oh, I'm sorry I missed it."

She grinned. "Well, you didn't. Her birthday is today. We're having a special dinner tonight, and we'd just love for you to join us."

He felt like a mouse in a room full of traps. "Is it a party?"

"No, just a small family dinner."

The trap snapped. Just mother, daughter and potential son-in-law, he guessed. There wasn't any easy way to escape, or at least one he could come up with quickly. He resented the part of his job that allowed people to take advantage of him.

"Sounds like fun." He choked the words out, knowing the evening with the church's two most persistent members would be anything but. Still, it was only a few hours. He could survive anything for a few hours.

Serena was surprised to see Andrew back at her door that afternoon, but when she let him in, he pushed past her on the way upstairs, carrying a wild-flower bouquet. Serena followed at his heels. He stopped at the doorway to Tessa's room and turned around, looking confused. The bedroom was empty.

Tessa bolted out of the bathroom. "Are you look-ing for me, Mr. Andrew? I brushed my teeth." She smiled to show the good job she'd done.

"Hello, Tess." He strode over and picked her up. "I'm glad you're feeling better today. I brought flowers for you."

"Aren't they pretty, Mommy? They're for me."

Andrew still looked confused when he lowered Tessa. She scampered off with her bouquet.

Serena motioned toward her child. "It's always like that. The fevers are gone by morning. And she usually feels fine."

Andrew shook his head. "I don't know how she could get from where she was last night to how she is today."

"Now that her condition has advanced to include joint swelling, the doctors told me, the fevers eventually will stop. That's why I wasn't prepared for it last night.''

He lifted an eyebrow. "You handled it like a pro."

"So did you—especially for a novice."

"I just followed your lead."

Her gaze caught with Andrew's and held. Their friendship today felt even stronger now that they'd survived at least one storm together. She only realized she was still looking at him when she felt a tug on the leg of her shorts.

"Mommy, can Mr. Andrew come to the park with us?"

"I'm sorry, sweetheart. He is probably busy. I'm sure he would come if he could."

Tessa moved to Andrew and turned on the charm. "Please come, Mr. Andrew. It will be really fun. Please. Please." She cocked her head in her best convincing pose.

Serena chuckled. He didn't stand a chance.

Andrew patted Tessa's head. "Maybe for a little while, but I have to go back to work after my lunch hour."

They pushed the umbrella stroller the five-minute walk to the park, but Tessa insisted on walking. The stroller would come in handy later when she was tired.

As soon as they entered the playground area, Tessa ran for the tire swing, with Andrew close behind. Tessa limped a little more today because of a swollen ankle joint, but it wasn't slowing her down, at least not yet.

Andrew spun Tessa until she was dizzy and then played with her in the sandpit a few minutes before joining Serena on the nearby bench.

"She's doing okay, isn't she?"

The way his brow furrowed showed he already knew the answer.

"You noticed the limp, didn't you?"

"I noticed."

Anxiety sneaked in to cloud the clear sky that had only been a fabrication, anyway. It was so much easier pretending everything was okay. "I don't know what they'll do at her next appointment."

"She'll be fine. I just know it. This spitfire won't let anything slow her down."

Serena wanted to believe him so much that she ached from the effort. But she'd seen so much evidence to the contrary. Agony had a way of stopping even Tessa.

Andrew stared at the huge mountain of sand Tessa was building. "God has watched out for her all along. I'm sure He's going to keep right on doing that."

Serena tried to stay on easy subjects—Tessa, doctors, the youth group—anything but the almost kiss. Had he realized now, as she had, how much of a mistake it would have been? And did he wish it had happened, anyway, as she did?

She pushed the thought away before it slipped out in her words. More humiliating than admitting how blown away she'd been would be discovering it hadn't bothered him at all.

"Did anything interesting happen at church today?"

"Charity popped into my office this morning and invited me to her mom's birthday dinner tonight."

"So what's the story with you and Charity?" Serena didn't like the tense feeling that nestled deep inside her. She had no right to be jealous. It shouldn't matter to her whom Andrew was involved with. Any single woman—without all the baggage she had—was a better choice. She knew it. Now she just had to fully accept it.

"No story," he said in an agitated voice. "And there's never going to be one."

His vehemence brought a smile to her lips. "She sure wants there to be a story. And who would blame her? Aren't you the most eligible bachelor in the church?" Her comment was barely out, and already she regretted saying it. What was wrong with her? Why was she baiting him?

The way he stiffened on the bench showed how little he appreciated her joke. "I'd gladly hand over that title to some other lucky guy. I'd heard of women going after men because of their money or fame—not that I'm saying either of those things is honorable. But I'd never heard of women whose lifetime goal was to marry a minister—even a youth minister or a music minister."

"Are you serious?" She studied him to see if he was. "Why would any woman in her right mind want to marry a minister? You mean there are women who beg to have their lives dictated by a congregation and to have their husband be responsible to so many people aside from their family?"

His grin faded quickly, as if her words had struck an uncomfortable chord in him. "That's not—at least, I hope that's not how they see it. I'd always guessed that these women simply were attracted to God-fearing men, but—" he paused to grin at her "—maybe I had it all wrong."

The banter was fun, but it only added to the forbidden curiosity that was building inside her. Did Andrew have someone in his life? Was that woman special enough to deserve someone like him? Serena didn't like the path her thoughts were hiking off to at such an alarming rate. She just couldn't picture any woman good enough for him.

"Even if you're avoiding the minister chasers, I bet there's someone out there who likes you for the Harley-riding ex-rebel that you are."

He was silent for a moment, then finally shook his head. "It's the job—women either come running, or hightail it."

Serena's jealous thoughts stopped cold. Pain reverberated off Andrew like sound waves, and she was shocked to feel his hurt and his loneliness as keenly as her own. She clasped her hands together to keep from comforting him with touch. "It sounds like you know that from experience."

He nodded and took on a distant look, staring across the playground to the tree-lined area that led to the Huron River. When he finally turned back to her, his eyes were damp. ''Marnie sure turned her tail and ran. She was my fiancée.''

''Fiancée?'' The word felt like fire to her throat.

''We'd dated through most of college, through the wild times.'' He shoved both hands back through his hair. ''She hadn't deserted me after the accident. I thought her staying meant something.''

Serena related completely to equating something less than full commitment and trust with love. She had scars to prove it. But, for the first time, she recognized scars in Andrew that were at least as deep as hers. Or deeper. ''No one could blame you for that mistake.''

Andrew continued without acknowledging her comment, as if the long-buried story was clamoring for a first telling. ''When I met Marnie, I was still running from my parents' God of fear and judgment. Then I caused the accident. In my guilt, I turned to the Lord of my own heart, a Father so perfect that He could forgive even me. Marnie wasn't pleased with this new development, but she must have figured it was a temporary habit, just as I believed that my example would lead her to a personal commitment.''

Andrew stopped for a moment, stepping over and admiring Tessa's impressive sandpit. He helped dig it a little deeper before sitting again. Serena needed time to take a breath, as well, to separate herself from his pain. But it became a heaviness, pressing on her shoulders and her heart.

"We were engaged and I'd completed a fellowship and been asked to join a clinical counseling practice, when I felt the call to ministry." His lips were a thin line as he stared down at the sand. "It was the strangest thing. My parents, who should have been thrilled by my choice, were openly skeptical of my motives. Marnie—she was spitting mad that I would choose God over her. She called the print shop to cancel the wedding invitation order that same afternoon I told her. Then she threw her engagement ring at me."

Her heart ached for him. Andrew, like her, had expected an awful lot from love. And they'd both learned painful lessons in human weakness. "How could she do such a thing to you, Andrew?"

Her words shocked her as much as they probably had him. They also produced a sense of déjà vu. She sounded just the way Andrew had when he'd reacted to her story about Trent. How could his fiancée have turned away from him after he'd announced his call to ministry? How could anyone leave Andrew Westin?

He stared at the curtain of trees again. "As horrible as it was, I know now it was the best thing for the both of us. I understood the scriptural warning not to be unequally yoked together with unbelievers, but I didn't think it applied to me, and if it did, I expected the Lord to give me a waiver."

"But God had other plans, didn't He. And the kids in the youth department should be really glad He did."

"I sure hope they are." Andrew stood suddenly. "I have to get back to church. I have to counsel someone this afternoon."

Counseling. She smiled at the thought of the counseling session that had initiated *their* friendship. They pushed Tessa home in the stroller, and Andrew took off in his car.

But the memory of his words refused to depart with him. Serena felt angry for the injustice done him, for the poor treatment of someone she was beginning to care a little too much about.

What right did she have to be this livid? It wasn't as if this other woman had taken away something that had been hers. She shuddered. If Andrew *were* hers, she would never... What good did it do to even think such a thing? It would never happen. It couldn't. They could be no more than friends, no matter how much she wished otherwise.

Even if she were free of her obligation to make her child the first priority, Andrew's ministry would make it difficult for him to become involved with a divorcée. Her mind connected with that truth, but her heart was having a hard time accepting it.

Chapter Eight

Some birthday party this had turned out to be. It was he and the Sims ladies, just as he'd predicted. Why hadn't they invited the Reverend Bob, so they could plan the ceremony right then?

Okay, it wasn't as horrible as that, but if he heard one more time what a great husband or wonderful dad he'd be, he might poke somebody with a dinner fork. He stared down at the utensil he'd use, the smaller dessert fork north of the fine china plate, southwest of the crystal goblet and just north of the matching silver spoon. Laura Sims had set the table as if royalty were visiting.

Hold on. The night is almost over. Saying those words over and over had helped at first, but even that was losing its therapeutic effect. There was one thing he couldn't figure out. If Laura believed her daughter was such a prize, why was she chatting up her qualities like an auctioneer at an estate sale?

"That apple pie smells wonderful, Charity. Don't you think so, Andrew?"

"It sure does," he responded halfheartedly, although his Benedict Arnold taste buds started watering.

Laura continued her sales pitch about her daughter's culinary prowess. He was tempted to break out into song. *Can she bake a cherry pie, Billy Boy, Billy Boy?* He swallowed a laugh.

The cooking, much of which he guessed was Laura's, anyway, was the only thing making this evening bearable, and even its effect was waning. He concentrated on apples and cinnamon, and on minutes ticking away as the conversation droned.

"What do you think of that new woman…Mrs. Jacobs?" Charity's voice was all syrup, but she emphasized the word *missus*.

Her words were no more inflammatory than anything else she'd said lately, but Andrew's blood pressure leaped. "Serena's a great help in the youth department. And I really admire her strength as she faces her child's illness." There was so much more he wanted to say—that she was beautiful when she smiled, that her compassion made him feel at peace with himself for the first time in his life, that he couldn't get her out of his mind. But he kept it all in the privacy of his heart.

"I'm sure she continues to need our prayers. It's amazing how quickly she's recovering from her divorce." Charity's feigned concern was transparent.

He had to get out of there before he said something he'd regret—or, worse yet, something he should regret but wouldn't. He declined Charity's offer of a stroll into the village for coffee and her unspoken promise of more cloying attention.

A woman like Charity couldn't possibly be what God had planned for his life. Not the compassionate God that Andrew knew intimately. Here he'd been pushing feelings for Serena away when she could be the person his Lord intended for him. At the very least, he was convinced he was the friend she needed. And he intended to spend a lot more time with her while he decided where their relationship might go.

He drove away from Charity's house, the anxiety in his heart decreasing as he put some distance between himself and those women. When he pulled his car into his drive, he eyed the fading red barn. Then he retrieved his riding boots and two helmets and jogged to the old building. It took a few kicks before the Harley roared to life, but when it did, he sat a few minutes, taking in the sound of the booming engine, the smell of burning fuel and the promise of freedom.

Twisting the throttle, he gave the machine just enough gas to maneuver it out of the barn. Then, when the path was clear, he opened the throttle. He sped forward into the wind, into the place where he felt closest to God.

As always in his life since the accident, he opened a prayerful dialogue as he pulled onto the road. He'd continue this open-eyed prayer until he reached his destination. By then, he hoped the Lord would have shown him His way.

"I don't know how you convinced me to do this," Serena yelled from the rear of the motorcycle.

Andrew kept his head forward but grinned as he turned onto Commerce Road. They were almost to the rural part of Milford Township, where he could finally go more than twenty-five miles per hour. He itched to feel that freeing speed, although he suspected even that rush wouldn't compare to the one he was experiencing now. Nothing could feel better than having Serena this close, her arms draped around his waist.

When he stopped at another annoying light, he turned his head to the side. "I didn't give you much choice."

"No, you didn't."

The light turned green, interrupting their conversation. Everything about this ride felt so right that he was glad he'd been persistent when he'd arrived with Hannah to baby-sit and Serena had looked at him with "no" written all over her face.

Once he'd convinced her that Tessa would be fine in Hannah's care and that he'd become a safe driver since the accident, he'd had the helmet on her in record time. Now he only wished he never had to take her home.

Delaying the inevitable, he took the long way around through Commerce Township before head-

ing back into Milford. He stopped in Central Park
and led Serena to the riverbank.

They sat in silence but not alone, as about a dozen
ducks swam near the shore. He felt sorry for the
birds. It was against village ordinance to feed them,
but they still came, hoping for a contraband meal.
He glanced at Serena and she smiled back. He felt
as hopeful as those silly birds.

No words were necessary with her. Being near her
and sensing her acceptance of him—just the way he
was—gave him a sense of completeness he'd never
felt before.

"When are you going to tell me what happened?" She propped her knees up and rested her
arms on them, appearing as if she had all the time
in the world to listen.

"I had to get away." He wanted to leave it at
that, but knew she'd never let him. "Dinner at the
Sims' house was, let's just say, a little pressure-
filled."

"Did Charity prove what a great little wife she'd
make? Could she make a cherry pie, Billy Boy, Billy
Boy?"

He laughed out loud. "Man, we must think alike.
I nearly broke out in song, except it was apple pie,
on the table in the middle of the china, crystal and
silver."

"China, crystal and silver? Hey, they're serious."

"You don't have to tell me that."

Serena's expression became somber. "You need
to tell Charity. You can't go on allowing her to be-

lieve that there's a chance with you, when it's impossible.''

''I know. I know. It's just that…it's not that easy.''

She smiled at him as she smacked at a mosquito. ''You're a coward.''

''That and I hate confrontation. Two small obstacles.''

He skipped a rock across the stream. One, two, three bounces before it sank. Serena tried to skip her own stone, which made a single plop.

''What was it really about tonight that upset you so badly?'' she asked finally.

The same tightness that he'd felt in his chest during that awful dinner returned. The air was being sucked right out of him. ''It's the expectations. I feel sometimes as if members of the church congregation believe I should be superhuman rather than just a servant who accepted God's call. They hold me up to this impossible ruler. I'll never measure up.''

She nodded. ''Are you sure it's them holding the ruler…and not you?''

He refused to believe that much pressure could come from inside him. It had to be others pressing him into the ground. ''I feel sometimes like they're searching for weakness, for flaws in me, so they can justify their own lack of commitment.''

''Your faith in God is strong, but you don't have any faith in people at all.''

The tightness increased, and he wondered suddenly if Serena's expectations, too, were more than he could handle. Anguish filtered through him, adding the weight of dread. "They haven't given me any reason to."

"Didn't your own transformation convince you of the human potential?"

It wasn't like that. Didn't she understand that he was nothing? Had always been nothing? "Only God can take the credit for making something out of me."

"But Andrew, *you* chose to let Him. You were responsible, in at least that way, for making the change. God would never have forced you into belief. He doesn't work that way, and you know it."

Something seemed to open up, allowing him to catch his breath. Maybe he'd made some small difference, but that didn't change his overall view. "But Mom and Dad gave me a really good primer into the heart of men. Even though they might, by now, accept that my conversion is real, they still check up on me regularly, waiting for me to fail."

"Not everyone is like your parents." Her words sounded clipped and angry. "Some people have it in their hearts to forgive, even to give second—and third—chances. Whatever happened to that man whom you injured in the accident? Did he forgive you?"

"Yeah, but John Bowley was a different breed." He fingered his cross, staring at the water. "After the accident, I visited him several times while he was undergoing physical therapy for his legs. I don't know how he could have forgiven me, but he had, even though he always walked with a limp after that.''

"Was he pleased when you made your commitment to God and accepted the call to ministry?"

Andrew felt the rush of pride that was always there when he thought of John. "He was so happy that he paid my tuition so I could return to school full-time. My cross necklace was a gift from John."

"He sounds like a great human being."

"He was. He's gone now, and I really miss him. He was more like a father to me than my own ever was."

Her surprised expression convinced him he'd said too much. Again. Why did he open himself like a filleted salmon every time he was around her? That was such a risk. If she truly knew him, he could forget about them being friends—or more. She'd probably run for her life.

"Doesn't John's forgiveness and his support at least give you a little faith in people?"

He wished it could. "He was just one man. I have so many examples of the cold, calculating creatures people can be." He read the disappointment in her rigid stance, in the way she briskly brushed invisible dirt off her jeans. It hurt as much as had any of the cutting comments his parents had ever made.

"If you opened your eyes, you'd see that there are just as many examples of good in people. They're God's creations. How can you question them?"

As he searched her eyes, opaque in the disappearing daylight, Andrew felt her frustration with him. He wished he could be the man she expected him to be. If only he could see the world as she saw it, with the bright eyes of childlike optimism. How had she managed to keep it, with all the curveballs life had tossed her? Serena was such an enigma to him, a puzzle he wanted to solve. She lived life intensely, loved fiercely and fought desperately for control. The third thing would have to give at some point, but even that intrigued him.

He lifted her hand, cradling it between his two, his wide fingers dwarfing her delicate ones. The warmth of her skin seemed to brand his, just as her spirit had touched his heart, affecting him in ways he was only beginning to understand.

"If I ever made a list of people worthy of my faith, you'd be right at the top."

The moment that had been fraught with emotion paled immediately next to this new intensity. The wooded backdrop to their river spot closed in around them until they seemed to be the only two people in the world.

Andrew watched his lungs expand with each inhalation and almost felt the blood pumping through his heart. He laced her fingers between his. They fit so well together, as if they'd touched before, if only in his dreams.

Serena closed her fingers over the back of his hand. It wasn't enough. The need to feel her within the circle of his arms became painful in his heart. He faced her, never releasing her fingers, and traced a line from her eyebrow to her chin with his other hand.

He startled her. Maybe she was as confused as he was about the fierce feelings that pirouetted between them. They were making him dizzy. Anxiety began low in his gut and spread. How could she trust, how could she believe, in a man who could never trust, was afraid to believe? Then Serena turned her face to his hand so that her lips lightly brushed his palm, and Andrew felt a rush of emotion such as he'd never known.

Settling her chin between his palms, he stilled there for a few seconds. Would she pull away? He couldn't control the tremor in his hands or the quiver unsettling his insides. It felt as if his future rested on the acquiescence or rejection of those beautiful lips.

Serena didn't move, except to lift the corners of her mouth into a smile. So honored, he touched his lips to hers in the sweetest, most gentle kiss of his lifetime. When he pulled away, he could only imagine returning to that point of perfection a million times more, knowing each visit would be as sweet as the first.

He leaned in once more, so close that he felt her soft breath on his chin. When he would have touched, a sound startled him, the high-pitched titter of a child's laughter, a child at the playground much too late at night. Serena stiffened, backing away a fraction of an inch. It felt like miles. She must have thought of Tessa then. Of responsibility. Their kisses couldn't share space with her higher calling.

As easy as it was to understand the reason for her reaction, it didn't wound him any less. Kissing her had felt like a homecoming in a life of always being on the run—from people, from feelings, from himself. Did he dare take a chance on the impossible now? Was he setting himself up for the greatest gain—or pain—he'd ever experienced?

The motorcycle ride back to Serena's apartment was chilly in more ways than one as the summer breeze turned cool. The emotional freeze, coming off Andrew in waves, frosted her soul. This was all her fault.

He bristled every time her fingertips brushed his sides, but she was afraid if she released him, she'd fall off the bike. There were so many other reasons she didn't want to let go of him. But he couldn't know them, and she couldn't allow herself to focus on them.

He was angry now, and she had no one to blame but herself. She should have listened to her intuition. It had told her what a mistake it would be to ride with Andrew, who'd shown up on her doorstep in worn jeans, black T-shirt and heavy boots.

She shouldn't have let him persuade her. Not with the collage of feelings that were melding so intimately with one another that she couldn't separate them. Comfort from his friendship and support. Desire to help him lead the church's youth. Pride over the tender way he cared for Tessa. Compassion for his personal pain. The need to find security in his arms.

It was so mixed up that she'd never make sense of it. She didn't even want to mouth the word that planted itself at the back of her mind with hearty roots. If she didn't say it aloud, she wouldn't have to deal with the incredible blow that such an emotion would throw at her well-planned life. She was beginning to find control again, and there was no way she'd give that up.

For a few seconds, she'd lost sight of what was most important. That other child's laughter had yanked her back to reality faster than a slap. Tessa was, and always would be, the center of her life. She couldn't let her needs as a woman get in the way.

But kissing Andrew— No. She couldn't allow herself to think about that. It had been confusing enough when they'd touched, and she'd fought herself not to wrap her fingers in the hair at his nape. When he'd pulled away from the kiss—or maybe she'd done it—she'd never felt so alone. How could she make herself forget what it was like kissing him?

He parked near the street lamp in front of her house and turned off the motorcycle's ignition. Could she even face him? The feelings were too recent, buried in a still-fresh grave. Her only alternative was to face the situation with as much dignity as she could muster and escape to deal with her confusion in private.

But the man who pulled off his helmet bore little resemblance to the one who'd kissed her as if she were made of glass. This man was hard. And angry. If she'd read that flash in his eyes correctly, he also was hurt.

"About…the park." She dragged her teeth across her bottom lip, trying to gather the courage to continue. "We need to talk about it."

Andrew watched the way she refused to meet his gaze and felt the squeeze in his heart tighten. She was about to blow him off. Well, if he'd learned nothing else in his miserable childhood, he'd mastered the art of survival. And often survival meant making the first strike. He flipped his hand to dismiss her words.

"It just happened. No big deal."

Was it hurt that tightened her features in the shadows before she straightened?

She planted her hands on her hips and shook her head. "Come on. You kissed me—I mean *we* kissed."

He couldn't understand why she was defending the moment. Did it give her some sick pleasure to rub salt in his wounds? "I said, 'No big deal.'"

Her actions seemed stiff—robotic even—as she climbed the steps, coming into the porch light. It had to be the yellow, artificial light that made her look pale.

She shook her head. "Whatever it was, it was also

a mistake. Neither of us was thinking straight. It had to be something—the ride or the breeze or the water…"

Or something altogether different. He wanted to say those words, but hadn't he suffered enough humiliation? If it meant nothing to her, then it would mean *less* than nothing to him—even if it killed him. He nodded his agreement.

Serena fidgeted with her hands. "We're friends, Andrew. But that's all we can be. Ever."

If her words had been a punch, he'd be down for the count. He ached all over, and she hadn't even poked him with a fingernail. This wasn't how it was supposed to work, and he was incensed he couldn't choose his reaction. He'd never have thought any woman—anyone at all—could monopolize his emotions this way. He didn't like it, wouldn't allow it.

Andrew shrugged, slipping on nonchalance as the armor he so badly needed. "Sure, we're friends. Good friends. I'm sorry about the kiss."

She smiled for the first time since they'd returned home. "Let's just forget about it, okay?"

He nodded, sorry that he had to lie. He'd have a talk with God about that one later. Defeated, he followed Serena into the house. Her change in demeanor was so sudden that it took him a minute to catch up. She expected him to play a role, and he wasn't about to disappoint her.

"Hi, Hannah, where's my favorite girl?"

Hannah chuckled, looking back and forth between Serena and Andrew quizzically. "I thought that was me. Oh, you mean Tessa. She and Sam, the tiger, have been asleep for at least an hour.''

Serena flitted across the room, picking up toys, straightening the comforter on the couch. ''Good, I'm glad you got her down. I was afraid she wouldn't go to bed.''

''No, she was perfect.'' Hannah paused, her faint smile drifting away as it always did when she wasn't entertaining Tessa. ''Did you guys have a nice ride?''

Serena nodded, leading them to the door. ''Yes…it was a lot of fun…riding the motorcycle. Now all I want to do is sleep. Good night.''

During the drive to the Woods' home, Andrew wondered if Hannah would comment about Serena's manner. She didn't. The teenager seemed to have too many of her own problems to notice anyone else's. The sadness, born of her mother's death, still pervaded her spirit. He needed to work harder to break through to Reverend Bob's unhappy daughter.

It was easier to focus his attention on a youth in need than to think of his own confusion, his wounded pride. At least he could put all of this restless energy to some use in helping Hannah face her sadness.

Still, a sense deep inside told him he was driving away from the very person who could help him heal his heart.

Chapter Nine

After they'd gone, Serena went upstairs to check on Tessa. She didn't want to wake her, but lingered by the bed to watch her sleep. Her child looked so peaceful.

Unable to watch her any longer without touching her, she lightly brushed Tessa's forehead and tucked two fingers beneath her neck just to be sure. Tessa was cool. The breath she'd held drained from Serena's lungs.

She tiptoed to the doorway. At least one thing in her life was as it should be. The rest of it was a mess. Tessa hardly moved in her sleep, so content was she in her dreams. Serena watched her, hoping her focus would hold at bay some of the other images dancing in her mind. But it failed as miserably as had her plan for keeping Andrew at arm's length.

She could still taste the sweetness of his kiss and could feel the security of being within the tight circle of his arms. Had she ever felt that safe before? Perhaps not, but she'd also never felt that out of control over her emotions and thoughts. She couldn't allow that. Control of this situation, if none of the others, was the only thing she had left.

Calling her feelings for Andrew "friendship" was like referring to her relationship with Tessa as "human to human." It didn't come close to characterizing the way her skin buzzed with new life the moment he walked into the room or the way her lungs constricted whenever he shot her a lopsided grin. Not to mention the way she longed to assuage his pain when he'd opened up to her.

But friendship was all she had to offer him—all she could bear to part with right now. Anything that took her mind off Tessa's health was an interruption, and an unwelcome one at that. Even if that weren't the case, opening her heart to Andrew would still be too great a risk. Sure, she'd known hurt before, but that pain was more from admitting she'd failed at marriage than from losing love.

Had she ever loved Trent? Real love that was more than companionship and a piece of the suburban pie? Had her heart ever cried out in misery when she'd been unable to comfort him? No, she didn't want to think about that. It would force her to turn some of the blame for her divorce inward, and she wasn't ready for that.

If she were that candid, she'd have to acknowledge that her heart *had* cried out over Andrew's pain, that a part of her seemed missing whenever he left the room. Even that the absent piece magically clicked into place when he knocked on her door. No, being honest with herself wasn't a good idea at all. She would have to admit that the biggest obstacle to her becoming closer to Andrew was fear. Would her heart ever heal, later, when she lost him?

Confused, she wondered if she should resign from her work in the youth department. It would make her life a lot easier. *Coward.* Since when did she take the easy way out? A commitment was a commitment, and she refused to bail out on hers—to the church, to the kids. She didn't care how uncomfortable she'd feel being near Andrew. Or how hard it would be to not wish for more.

On Sunday, Serena decided that commitments weren't all they were cracked up to be. She scanned the blank faces in the junior high Sunday School class. Had anyone gotten the lesson she'd been presenting for the past thirty minutes?

"How can we behave like Job in our daily lives?"

She held her breath and hoped for an answer. Any answer that would show Job's Old Testament story of woe had broken through the fidgeting and giggling.

"By trusting in God no matter how much bad stuff happens in our lives."

The answer was a shock, especially coming from Steffie Wilmington, who'd spent much of the class peeking at Brendan Hicks. Maybe the kids were learning something, after all.

"And why is that hard to do?" Serena waited the requisite two minutes before anyone even raised a hand. Then it was Brendan, the object of so many junior high school affections, who lifted his hand.

"Because it's so hard to let go of control." He elbowed Chuck Donovan and continued whatever joke they'd shared before the question.

Serena clamped her teeth together to keep her jaw from falling open. Why was it so easy for a kid to understand the very thing she struggled with every day? She recognized the problem. But knowing it intellectually wasn't enough. Like her, these children realized they should give God control. But they hadn't seen enough of the world's misery to understand her struggle.

Could it be as simple as Brendan made it seem in his one-sentence answer? The question followed her as she dismissed in prayer, retrieved Tessa from 'Tiny Tots' and found a pew in the center of church where they'd started sitting lately. It was better to stay away from the back pews that were usually filled with whispering teens.

Today, though, the middle seemed way too close to the front of the church and to Andrew, who smiled at everyone in the congregation, except for her. He sported a crisp navy suit, white shirt and a not-so-subtle tie with splashes of navy and red.

Still, he looked miles away from the ultra-masculine driver who'd wheeled her around on his motorcycle before stealing her reason with his kiss. This was church. She wouldn't think about *that* here. Or anywhere for that matter. Anymore.

"'Shall we gather at the river.'" Tessa sang the only words she remembered from the well-known hymn.

Serena looked down at her daughter, who was grinning up at her. The sound of Tessa's sweet voice made Serena realize that until that moment, she'd only been mouthing the words. Her spiritual life had been like that lately; she was just going through the motions. That had to stop. She was here for worship, not to worry about a kiss—even if it had changed everything and there was no way to change it back.

Reverend Bob required her attention as he began his sermon on Ruth and Naomi. "Ruth told her mother-in-law, '…for where you go I will go, and where you lodge I will lodge; your people shall be my people, and your God my God.'"

Serena could have recited that story from memory, detailing Ruth's brave decision to turn her back on her family and embrace Naomi and her God. So why did it hit her so hard today? Would she ever know the kind of faith Ruth had?

She prayed she would. *Lord, show me the right path and give me the strength to follow it, no matter where it leads.*

If she were a better person, she would pray that the Father would take control of her life. She couldn't bear to be that dishonest, though. She wasn't ready for that. After Tessa's condition was under control and Serena had tied her own emotional turmoil in a neat little bundle, maybe then she would be ready.

Andrew's heart quickened as Serena and Tessa approached in the greeting line next to the church exit. He was exhausted from trying not to look at her during the service, and here she was again. It was just more proof that life wasn't fair.

When he finally allowed his eyes to drink in the sight of her, he was afraid he'd never be able to look away. She looked prettier than ever. Her hair was all tied up in some sort of clip, showing the smooth curve of her neck. She wore her multicolored dress and was bare-legged with sandals, prompting an image in his mind of her running barefoot in that dress along the water's edge.

His straying thoughts stopped cold when he looked at her face. She looked more fragile today. Dark circles ringed her eyes and trapped him with guilt. He was partially responsible for putting those circles there. If she'd clocked as little sleep as he had the past few nights, it was a wonder that either of them was standing upright.

When he shook her hand, he felt a slight tremor in it. Had it been his hand or hers? And was it a flash of intensity he'd read in her eyes, or was he projecting his inappropriate feelings on her?

Next to him, Mrs. Brewster chatted with Reverend Bob about the secret family recipe potato salad she'd bring to today's church picnic at Camp Dearborn. His exhaustion doubled at the thought of that afternoon-into-evening event, even though he'd looked forward to it for weeks.

He was still tearing his gaze from Serena, who'd moved on to greet Reverend Bob, when he felt a tug on the bottom of his suit jacket. So grown-up that it made his heart ache, Tessa outstretched her hand for a proper handshake. Instead he bent and lifted her to rest on his hip. "How's it going, Tess?"

At least one Jacobs female was happy to see him. She giggled as she looked down at the other mere mortals from her perch.

"Will you be at the picnic? Mommy says we can go."

He rubbed noses with her. "If you'll be there, you can bet I will, too. Are you going swimming with me?"

She nodded enthusiastically. "Can we play chicken? That was fun."

"Sure, I can't wait." When he would have expected some other exciting plans to come out of her mouth, Tessa suddenly looked as if her birthday had passed without presents or a cake. "What's wrong, sweetheart?"

"I have to go to the doctor in two tomorrows. Mommy says they're going to poke me. I hate pokes."

"Yeah, I hate them, too. But they're over pretty quick, right?"

She stuck out her bottom lip. "They still hurt."

"That's why nurses give you prizes when they're done. What do you get?"

"Stickers. Lots of stickers. And sometimes cool stuff like balls or coloring books."

He looked over her shoulder at Serena, who stepped closer. "Wow, you're lucky."

"I cry sometimes, but I told Mommy that I promise not to cry when I get poked this time."

Squeezing her extra hard, he glanced at Serena. Her eyes glistened with unspent tears. His own throat tightened. He couldn't remember the last time he'd cried for any reason, yet this little girl trying to be tough was enough to reduce him to very unmasculine sobs. What was happening to him? Everything inside of him had turned to mush since meeting Serena.

Feeling nothing had been easier. Emotion equaled pain. He was spiraling toward that end as surely as water swirled down a drain. And there didn't seem to be anything he could do to stop it. How strange it seemed that he didn't even want to.

So far, the picnic that afternoon had gone better than Andrew ever would have predicted. But as he dished up some banana pudding at the serving table, he knew his good fortune had just run out.

"Oh, Andrew, you naughty boy," Laura Sims drawled. "You haven't even tried Charity's devil's food cake. It's decadent." She took a bite of the sweet concoction and rolled her eyes.

"You're wrong, Sister Laura. Tessa and I had

some earlier. We even took a piece back to her mother.''

The haughty expression on Laura's face over his mention of Serena would have been enough to make the picnic worthwhile, but he'd already had a great time in the water with Tessa and the youth group. Charity approached, seeming to catch the end of his comment. It felt as if his facial bones would break if he didn't smile, but he held back. Guilt trickled in then, making him shoot up a prayer to be more charitable.

The day would have been perfect if he could have spent more time with Serena and Tessa, just the three of them. What a useless thought. He tucked it in the back of his mind.

He made his way back to the volleyball net, where competition continued between parents and teens. He'd already played awhile, with Serena on the opposite side in a boys-against-the-girls challenge. He grinned, remembering what a lousy player Serena was.

He hadn't been constantly monitoring Serena, but he'd sensed her movement from one activity to the next. As she sat on a blanket next to her sleeping child, he focused his attention on her. She appeared so sweetly in her element—simply a woman and mother at peace in her world. The ache in his heart struck so swiftly that he squeezed his arm against his chest to dull the pain.

He wanted to be a part of that world. But he'd have to settle for a whole lot less. For now. Maybe for always. Even that knowledge didn't stop the force that pulled him to her. He searched for a plausible excuse with each step that drew him nearer. Maybe he'd suggest a game of lawn darts—

Charity caught him just before he reached the blanket. "I've been waiting to play lawn darts with you all day, Andrew." Her smile was flirtatious and victorious.

Seeing no easy escape, he followed her. Still he peeked at Serena as he passed. Was she even the slightest bit jealous? But she stared toward the man-made lake, her thoughts probably miles away from him or his unfortunate feelings for her.

Charity had thoroughly beaten him by the time he headed to the outdoor sanctuary—consisting of lawn chairs, blankets and a small stage—for the evening service. Reverend Bob had even let him off the hook, telling him he could sit out in the congregation. He headed for the spot Serena and Tessa had claimed, hoping to be invited to join them.

"Mr. Andrew, Mr. Andrew! Sit here." Tessa patted a place beside her on the blanket.

He'd have to remind himself to kiss the munchkin for that later. Trying not to notice the way Serena shifted on the blanket and smoothed it with her hand, he plopped down on the ground and drew Tessa onto his lap. He didn't care about the odd looks that were probably being focused on his back from a few in the congregation. He caught Serena giving him a sidelong glance and grinned.

"Do you work in two tomorrows?" Tessa whispered.

"Do you mean Tuesday? I usually do, but not this week because I have to work Monday. What do you have in mind?" He remembered her doctor's appointment but wasn't sure what she was suggesting.

"Will you go to see the doctor with us?"

Her request tore at his heart. There was no reason that a four-year-old should have to know about needles, ultrasounds and bone marrow biopsies. Could he bear to see her in pain that way, especially after that night with the fever? But if it would make her feel better having him there, he'd be there, no matter what.

"It sounds like fun, but we'd better talk to your mom about that."

"Mommy, Mr. Andrew's coming to the doctor with us."

Serena raised an eyebrow. "We'll talk about that after the evening service."

Andrew tried to concentrate on Reverend Bob's sermon. How would Serena try to get out of this one? But he couldn't worry about that now, not while they were worshipping outside, right in the middle of God's creations.

At the close of the service, they joined in a circle to sing "We Are One in the Bond of Love." He'd never felt the hymn's lyrics more strongly than he did there, gripping Serena's fine-boned hand on one side and Tessa's tiny one on the other. There was a bond between himself and Serena, no matter how much they tried to deny it. And Tessa fit perfectly within it.

After the last words were sung, Serena turned to him. "It's not necessary for you to go with us to the hospital. That will be an all-day thing Tuesday, and I know how busy you are, so it—"

"I'd like to go." He grabbed two corners of the picnic blanket and helped her fold it.

"You'll be awfully bored. Tessa has an appointment in the morning with pediatric rheumatology and one in the afternoon with pediatric ophthalmology. That doesn't even include blood work or X rays if they're ordered."

"Then, I'll keep you both company."

She bit her lower lip and busied herself packing the picnic basket. She glanced around until her gaze caught on Tessa. Like always, she'd superglued herself to Hannah's side.

"What did you already tell her?"

It was the first time he realized Serena hadn't been privy to their conversation. His ticket past her misgivings could come in the retelling of that discussion, provided he treaded carefully. "I told her it sounded like fun." Okay, so it wasn't everything he'd said, but it was the most germane part.

She shook her head in an obvious sign of defeat. "You're sure you want to be there?"

"Of course I'm sure. Why wouldn't I be?"

She looked at him as if she wasn't confident he'd be there, and he tried not to take her lack of belief personally. That was another man's crime, not his.

On the day of Tessa's most crucial test, her former husband had failed her and Serena on so many levels aside from fidelity.

Her worries weren't directed at him. But that didn't make the fact that she was having them sting any less. Didn't she realize it was *him* she was talking to, not this failure of a man from her past? He wasn't the type of man who would turn his back on her. Ever. Couldn't she see that?

If she were his, he'd see to it that she never had to worry again.

Chapter Ten

Do you really think you're strong enough? That question and twenty others like it tormented Andrew while he finished cleaning up the church picnic site. Trailed by his own accusations, he headed, exhausted, to his car.

As much as he wished it, could he really be the man that Serena and Tessa needed? Could he pick them up when they fell, cradle them when they were scared? A creeping sense of dread filled him. Would he fail them the way he had failed everyone else he'd ever loved?

"Hey, Andrew."

He didn't have to turn around to know that vapid voice—the one Charity affected whenever she was around him. If she only wouldn't try so hard, act so desperate, she probably wouldn't be so lonely. He wished he knew how to tell her that.

"Hi, Charity. How's it going?"

"Okay, except I'm stranded." She shrugged, not looking at all unhappy. "Mother—I don't know what she was thinking. She packed up the car and left without me."

"I guess we'd better get you home, so you'll be there when your mother discovers she's missing a passenger."

She waved away his comment. "I'm sure she won't worry. She knows I'm resourceful enough to find a ride."

Resourceful enough to con your way into a ride, you mean. He was angrier with himself than with her that he'd allowed this to happen. What choice did he have? If he told her to find another way home, she'd come off as a distressed damsel and he, a far cry from the Good Samaritan. Still, there had to be some limit to how accommodating he was required to be.

A while later he pulled into Charity's driveway and left the car running. He stared at the steering wheel and waited. She didn't say anything, didn't reach for the door. Nothing.

Andrew couldn't take it any longer. He glanced at her. Charity sat observing him as if he were some amazing discovery. He felt trapped by the silence. Would she say something clever, something that would change this from the most uncomfortable moment in his life?

Instead, she leaned forward and kissed him awkwardly. He recoiled against the driver's-side door in shock.

"I've wanted to do that for months." Her voice had a new edge of vulnerability.

She opened the door, but he put a hand on her arm. "Charity, wait." She turned to him expectantly, but he grabbed her by both shoulders to make her listen and to keep her from acting again. "That can't—won't—happen again. You're a great woman, but I can't give you the type of relationship you're looking for."

He released her, but instead of retreating, she crossed her arms in a belligerent pose.

"You don't have any idea what I'm looking for, what I want or need. You can't take your eyes off our sweet little divorcée long enough to even look at me. I wonder what she's offering to keep you so interested."

Anger hit him so hard and fast that his world blurred. He grabbed the steering wheel and squeezed hard. "I don't care what you say about me, but don't you say anything bad about Serena. Ever."

"Whatever you say." She slammed the car door, stalking toward the house. An observer would have thought that Charity had been accosted—not the other way around.

He couldn't get out of her driveway fast enough. He wanted to get as far away as possible from this woman who pointed her finger at everyone else's shortcomings without ever examining her own heart. She reminded him so much of two people in his past. He hated reminders of his parents, and she made him as furious as they once had.

Andrew drove home confused. Charity's unfortunate advance shouldn't have had an impact on him, and yet it propelled him as nothing else could have. He had to make sense of it, somehow. With the Lord's help, he would.

Only one thing was clear to him: the only time his world seemed sane was when Serena was with him.

Dread weighted Serena's head on her pillow when she awoke Tuesday morning. It was still there as the time drew near for them to leave for the hospital. Her stomach rolled. That bit of toast and coffee had been a mistake. This felt so much like another morning in her past, and that first time had taken all of her reserves to overcome. She wasn't sure she could survive it this time.

He's not coming. Again. She shook her head, trying not to become nostalgic. Andrew wasn't Trent. He was nothing like the man who'd walked away. Andrew was a stick-around kind of guy. She knew it, but the frayed edges of her confidence continued to pull away in tiny strings. He'd promised. That should have been enough. But it wasn't.

Would she ever learn to trust again, to place her comfort or happiness in another's hands? She'd begun to do that with Andrew, and yet here she sat, waiting and constantly checking her wristwatch. Just like before. *If he was coming, why was he fifteen minutes late?*

"Mommy, is Mr. Andrew here yet?" Tessa stood next to her, peeking out the front window.

"No, honey, he isn't." She searched for the words. How could she tell her hopeful little girl that he wasn't coming? How could Tessa possibly understand that another man she loved wouldn't come through for her? That wasn't how Serena wanted her child to see life, as a place where trust was only for saps. She wanted her to count on people, to be open to the good they could bring to her life. How could she convey that message while explaining that Andrew was a no-show? "I'm sorry, sweetheart, but he—"

"Don't worry, Mommy. He'll be here in a few minutes."

With a certainty that Serena wondered if she herself could ever feel, Tessa flitted off to her room for a few more minutes of play. Undoubtedly, she'd jump on the bed and mess up her two perfect pigtails.

Serena glanced out the window again, as she paced the area between the coffee table and the sofa. She closed her eyes and prayed for hopeless things and for the preservation of her child's innocent faith. As she opened her eyes, she saw Andrew pulling his car to the curb. He trotted up the steps, looking as harried as she felt.

Yanking the screen door open, Andrew held his hand up to stop her tirade. "Before you say anything, I just want you to know how sorry I am that I'm late. I was on my way out the door when Rev-

erend Bob called and wanted to talk about 'things.'
I got off the phone as quickly as I could.''

From the nervous way he licked his lips and focused on the wallpaper, she didn't have to ask if
those "things" involved her. After the little familial
scene the two of them had made Sunday at the
church picnic, there were sure to be some questions
among congregation members. Funny, she'd just
prayed for his arrival, and now she couldn't bring
herself to look at him.

"You didn't believe I'd show."

Serena jerked her head to meet his gaze. The hurt
she read there burned like a festering wound. "I'm
sorry. I have this history, and it's hard not to fall
into old habits."

He pressed his lips together, jaw tightening. "I
was late. That's my only crime. For that I apologize.
I would never fail to show up without a very good
reason."

"Andrew, I was wrong—"

"No." Anger danced in his eyes. "Let me finish.
For every mistake I make in our friendship, I will
take full responsibility. But I refuse to be held ac-
countable for someone else's sins."

He stuffed his hands in the pockets of his jeans
shorts. "I can't carry that much weight. It's too
heavy for anybody."

Tessa saved Serena from an answer she didn't
have by whizzing past her and into Andrew's arms.
Serena was so glad her daughter's faith had been

confirmed. She only wished she could believe that way. She felt the failure of knowing she couldn't.

Andrew and Tessa chatted happily as they headed to her car. She grabbed Tessa's backpack and followed them out, catching only the tail end of their conversation.

"I promise I won't cry when I get poked." Tessa pointed to the bend of her arm where it always hurt.

Andrew lifted her chin and stared into her sad eyes. "You can cry all you want to. I'll even cry with you if you want me to."

Tessa's merry giggle was worth every bit of Serena's worry and the stomach upset. Maybe Andrew coming along wasn't such a bad idea. If it took Tessa's mind off needles and the strange bending and twisting of limbs during her exam, then it was a great idea.

They got into the car and headed for the hospital. Serena had only turned the car off Milford Road onto Interstate 96 before Tessa fell asleep in her car seat, leaving her and Andrew alone to their silence.

A lot of backpedaling was in order after their earlier confrontation, so Serena started with light conversation. "The picnic was nice the other night."

He stared out the window. "It was a lot of fun."

"Didn't you give Charity a ride home?" The words were out of her mouth before she could stop them. The jealousy that inspired them tasted bitter. If she couldn't afford the risk of making him a part of her life, she had no right to ask him about his.

"Why do you ask?"

He was watching her now. She sensed it before she peeked to confirm her suspicion. She checked her rear-view mirror and side mirrors for something to do.

"Just making conversation."

"As a matter of fact, I did. It seems that Laura packed up her car and drove away, *accidentally* forgetting her daughter."

"That sounds like some big accident." Her tone sounded like a growl, even to her.

Andrew choked back laughter but finally surrendered to it. Unable to resist, she joined in until her eyes were damp.

"It really was kind of bad." He paused, becoming serious. "When we got to her house, instead of getting out of the car, she kissed me."

An ache formed inside her heart, that said *she* should have been the only one kissing Andrew. But she'd made it clear they wouldn't be kissing again. Now she mourned that loss. She tried to shake away the image of his lips against her own. She could still feel the pressure, the sweetness. The warmth remained even when the thought retreated to her subconscious, where it belonged.

Andrew continued as if he didn't recognize her internal battle. "It was as humiliating for me as it was for her. I told her that couldn't happen again, that I wasn't the man she needed. But she made it worse by saying that I couldn't know what she needed because my attention was too focused on someone else."

The shiver that started somewhere low on Serena's spine fluttered up her neck and to her scalp. Both of them were well aware of who that "someone else" was. They needed to talk about it—soon, but not now.

She took the coward's way out and changed the subject. "Are you sure you didn't encourage Charity?"

His left hand clenched the console. "I did everything but put a sign on my forehead that read 'Not Interested'—just as you have with me."

Serena opened her mouth to respond but couldn't find the words. Didn't he see how he'd misread those signs? She wanted to tell him about feelings that were ill-advised but still very real. She just couldn't. It was too much of a risk. But need was battling with risk in a death match. She wasn't sure how much longer she could resist telling him the truth.

For the second time that day, she escaped from responding when the answers would have incriminated her. This time it was the University of Michigan Medical Center's buildings that provided a reprieve as they came into view. In various shapes, the brick buildings jutted out of the otherwise green landscape.

Right now Serena needed to concentrate on parking at the Taubman Center next to C.S. Mott Children's Hospital and getting Tessa to the pediatric specialties office. Later she'd focus on Tessa's checkup at the W.K. Kellogg Eye Center across campus.

All that activity would leave little time for worrying about the upcoming conversation with Andrew. But that talk would come later, she was sure. Andrew wouldn't let such an important issue lie. And if she were honest with herself, she'd admit that she didn't really want him to. They had to decide what to do about the attraction and growing feelings that bubbled between them, threatening at any moment to boil over.

Serena curled into an upright version of the fetal position in her hospital waiting room chair. Andrew wanted to take her in his arms so badly that he paced to keep his hands to himself. He was thankful that Tessa was too busy playing at the activity table to notice her mother's distress. Dressed in a paisley hospital gown while she waited her turn in X ray, she concentrated on using a magnet to move a tiny car through a sand maze.

"I still can't believe they want me to give her shots."

Since Serena didn't seem to be talking to him, he didn't answer. But he gave in to his need and sat next to her again, this time reaching over to pat her hand. He held his breath, waiting for her to pull away. She didn't. He was grateful for the way she squeezed his hand in return. It had been hard enough accepting that she'd believed he wouldn't show up that morning. Her pulling away from his compassion would have put him over the edge.

Couldn't she see that he was as faithful as a Saint Bernard and a lot less smelly? He was nothing like the other man who hadn't shown up and then had walked away. If she didn't realize that, then she didn't know him at all.

She couldn't see it, or she'd never have looked as pale as she had when he'd arrived. Instead of getting angry, he had to help her see the truth. That meant being what she needed right now and forgetting about his own needs. Serena's focus had to be on the child, so he planned to place his on supporting the mother.

She turned in the seat until she faced him, pulling her hand away. "How am I going to do that?"

It took him a second to realize that she was still talking about giving injections. "You'll do what you have to, just as you've done all of Tessa's life."

She buried her face in her hands. "I won't be able to do it."

Andrew glanced at Tessa, who was still engrossed in the table activity. It wouldn't help for her to see her mother so upset. He pulled Serena's hands from her face. "You gave great saline injections to the shot dummy."

She smiled halfheartedly. "Just because I can shoot saltwater into a huge wristwatch made of the same stuff as the old toy Stretch Armstrong doesn't mean I can stick a needle in my daughter. What if I hurt her?"

He folded her hands between his. "I know you don't want to see her in pain from the joint swelling. And from what the pediatric rheumatologist said, these injections of methotrexate might help control her condition. You want that, right?"

She nodded. "But what if I can't hold her down? I'll end up poking us both."

"Don't worry about that. I'll come tomorrow, and every Wednesday until you feel comfortable, to help you hold her for the injection." He squeezed her hands again. "You saw what a good job I did today at the blood lab, holding her still. I'm a natural at this."

That promise was easy to make. Too easy. It wouldn't be a hardship to make himself available to assist her with weekly injections, when he wanted to be near her all the time, anyway.

That realization was terrifying. What kind of pain was he setting himself up for—letting his heart get tangled up over a woman who wasn't ready for anything more significant than a good friendship?

He shouldn't have allowed Serena so far into his heart, but there was nothing he could do to keep her from burrowing deeper still. He had to make it stop. He needed to hold on to what was left of his good sense, because this woman and her sweet little girl were threatening to become something his parents had never tried hard enough to be with him: a family.

The temptation to sit back and let the worst happen was becoming greater each day. If wanting something badly enough could cause it to happen, then they'd already be a legal family and setting up housekeeping. He should know better. He'd spent a lifetime wishing for the impossible.

Lord, please make me understand Your will here. I want so much to take care of them, love them, but it needs to be Your will and not mine. Also, please hold Tessa close to Your heart. She needs You.

Andrew stared at the ceiling. Had God even heard his pleas? Could He sense his desperation? Maybe He was just taking his time in answering.

Chapter Eleven

Andrew wasn't all that surprised when Reverend Bob called him into his office Wednesday morning. In fact, he should have predicted the meeting, based on their telephone conversation of the day before.

It had to have been out of nervousness, then, that he recounted his performance on assignments from the past week. He'd taken the Lord's Supper to the senior center, led the women's Bible study and done the rounds for the hospital ministry.

As far as he could tell, he hadn't dropped the ball even once. So as he sat in Reverend Bob's office, waiting for his return, he contemplated the one subject they would discuss. Or rather, the one person. If only there was a way for him to escape that conversation again. But Reverend Bob marched through the door before he could think of one.

"Great, Andrew, you're here." He crossed to his

desk and sat behind it. "Now we'll have a chance to talk."

But they didn't talk. Not really. Bob danced around subjects in big, swirling loops. Andrew wasn't about to stop the music, either—not when he could delay the discussion a little longer. Finally, Bob quit on his own, bringing up the matter that weighed heavily between them.

"Are you and Mrs. Jacobs seeing each other socially?"

Andrew swallowed hard. Why did he feel as if he were defending his life? "Are you asking if we're dating? No, we're not. We're friends, though. And if you want to know if I wish we were dating, I'd tell you 'yes.'"

"I see." Reverend Bob sat with his elbows on the desk, his hands folded together and thumbs pressed to his lips. "Serena is a kind, lovely woman. She has struggled with many difficulties, especially her divorce. But right now, the one I'm interested in is you."

Andrew crossed his arms. "I'm fine."

"Why are you considering the hardest path when you could find an easier—or less complicated—one? There are so many ladies who've never been married you could date and that who wouldn't cause friction in our congregation."

Andrew's face felt hot. His insides burned. "Are you really recommending that I take the easy road? That's not at all what you preach from the pulpit."

"This is entirely different, and you know it."

Andrew held back his anger. Reverend Bob was more than his spiritual guide; he was a friend. So Andrew forgave him for being so wrong.

"Some people might have a problem with Serena being divorced, but I don't." Andrew shook his head to emphasize his point. "I have no idea what the Father has planned for us, but I feel He is leading me to be there for Serena—maybe even to be *with* her."

Reverend Bob lowered his head. "I'm sorry. I shouldn't have said what I did. I have performed plenty of second marriages, and I never would have done it if I didn't believe their vows would be blessed."

Andrew waved away the comment when the Reverend finally looked up. "Forget it. You were trying to protect me. But remember this, I know what I'm doing. God is leading here."

The minister leaned forward. "There's something you should know, though. A certain young church member called me, concerned about how Mrs. Jacobs might affect your soul."

"How many guesses do I get as to who this young lady is?"

Reverend Bob smiled ruefully. "I think one would be plenty. I'm afraid Miss Sims has her sights set on you, and she won't be easily dissuaded."

Andrew shivered at the memory of that unfortunate kiss, but he didn't mention it. "We had a discussion Sunday night, and I believe she understands now."

"She called me just yesterday. She's used to getting her way, to having her mother give her anything she wants."

Andrew nodded. Turning his back on Charity was a bad idea. She probably was very angry. He sensed he'd regret offending her. How much, he didn't know.

Serena heard the knock at six o'clock, just as Andrew had promised. Tessa had the front door open before she could make it out from the kitchen.

"Mr. Andrew's here! Do you want to watch *Veggie Tales* with me?" Then Tessa shrieked.

Her nerves already stretched tight, Serena rushed toward the entry. That was all she needed—another bad twist in a rotten day. At the door, Tessa was dancing around as if it were Christmas. And standing beside Andrew was her gift: Hannah.

"Mommy, you didn't tell me Hannah was babysitting!"

Serena raised an eyebrow at Andrew. He only grinned at her. She was so glad he was there. "It was kind of a surprise."

Tessa dragged Hannah off to the television.

"Are you ready?" Andrew stepped toward her, so close it appeared he would touch her arm.

He didn't, but she almost felt a reassuring squeeze, anyway. "As ready as I can be."

She led him to the kitchen where she'd stashed the supplies—syringes, alcohol swabs, two tiny vials of medicine, even a plastic sharps disposal container.

"Well, here goes." She swabbed off the top of one vial with alcohol, inserted the syringe into the top and inverted it to withdraw the oily, yellow liquid. Everything would be okay if she could just keep from thinking. Going through the motions had to be enough, because it was all she had.

"You're doing fine," Andrew told her. "You see, you're handling this like a pro."

She didn't want to talk about it because that would lead to thinking. She needed to change the subject. "That was a nice touch to bring Hannah along. I'm sure her visit made Tessa's day."

"I didn't do it for her."

Serena looked up from her focus on flicking air bubbles in the syringe. Then she remembered. They'd agreed to go out for coffee after the shot. How had she let him talk her into that? Frustrated by a bubble that refused to budge, she squirted all of the medicine back into the vial and started over. Would she ever become proficient at this?

"Maybe it's not a good idea to leave Tessa after she's just had her first shot. She'll probably need me." She flicked until the last tiny bubble disappeared.

"Tessa will be fine—once the shot is over. Besides, she has Hannah here to play with, and I've hired Hannah to sit for a few hours."

He paused, looking at her so deeply that her skin

seemed no barrier to his seeing what was happening inside her.

"I'm worried about *you*. You're going to need some tender care after this, and I'm just the guy to give it to you."

Tender care. It sounded so good. And it had been so long since she'd had that. Who was she kidding? No one—aside from her mom and dad—had attended to her that way, made her feel precious…ever. "We'll see" was all she could give him. No matter how much she yearned for someone to lean on, her needs came second.

She capped the syringe and put it aside, having Andrew stretch out his arm so she could practice one more time. Pinching the skin on the back of his arm, she tried to feel the difference in tissue between the fat layer, to which she'd have to administer injections, and the muscle layer. She hoped that knowledge would transfer when she attempted the same thing on Tessa's back end.

When they returned to the living room, Serena held the syringe and alcohol swab behind her back. "Hey, Tessa, it's time for your shot now. Let's do this really fast."

Tessa screamed and ran for the front door, but Andrew caught her easily and whirled her about as if that were just part of a fun game.

"If you try to be really still, it will be over so fast you'll barely know it," he promised.

"No, no, Mommy! I don't want a shot!"

She couldn't do it. How could she purposely

cause her child more pain? Serena steadied her
body, even if her insides refused to follow suit. She
would do this because she had to. Because a little
pain now might control the agony Tessa was so used
to, that she hardly complained.

Andrew placed Tessa belly-down on the floor facing the television for a distraction. Serena worked
quickly, lowering Tessa's shorts, swabbing the spot,
and lifting the skin in what she hoped was the right
place. Andrew held down Tessa's kicking legs.

Tessa's pleas filled Serena's head, and her hand
trembled as she pierced her daughter's skin and released the medication. She withdrew the empty syringe, feeling just as depleted. Being the stand-up
grown-up this time felt like an impossible challenge.

She looked up to see Andrew straightening
Tessa's pants and cradling her in his lap. Already,
her shrieks had calmed to soft whimpers. She didn't
beg for Mommy, but buried her face deeper into
Andrew's chest. Warmth spread through Serena's
heart as she witnessed the moment of tender compassion. Andrew was there. He was always there.
She could get used to that.

Serena sipped her coffee at Klancy's diner an
hour later, her hands and insides still quivering. "I
can't imagine going through that every week for the
next few years. I'm not strong enough."

Andrew laid his hand on hers. "You're stronger
than you think. It was hard, but you did what you
had to do."

"I did, didn't I." At least she could give herself that. She scanned the brightly papered walls and the mostly empty vinyl-covered booths. Andrew had convinced her to come here after Tessa had magically jumped from his arms and begged to watch the rest of her video with Hannah.

"I guess I should feel lucky that she isn't a juvenile diabetic. I don't know how those parents deal with giving multiple injections every day."

He smiled at her and squeezed her hand. "The same way you do what is necessary—with love for their kids and a lot of prayers."

Prayers. Had she prayed even once today? Another failure in a life overflowing with them. "Sometimes I forget to pray for God's help and later forget to thank Him for the help He gave, anyway."

"Serena, doesn't it get really heavy sometimes?"

She didn't understand his words, but she felt the absence of warmth when he removed his hand from hers. She had no doubt his pulling away was about more than the silver-haired waitress's appearance to offer coffee refills. "I'm not sure what you mean."

"Balancing the whole world on your shoulders?"

She clasped her hands in her lap. "That's not fair." If she'd been supporting the whole planet, its weight had suddenly tripled.

Andrew straightened. "No, and life isn't fair, either. You've already discovered that. And on some level you have to know that you can't control any of this, but you're killing yourself trying. Can't you see that you're spitting into the wind?"

The sting of his words crept through several layers of emotional protection. What could she say to someone who'd so perfectly diagnosed the mess that was her life? Why did she strain so hard to capture the reins when it was apparent they'd forever elude her grasp? Was it because not trying meant failing to give her best for Tessa? Or was she just a fool?

She gripped the edge of the table, trying to steady her hands and her thoughts. Soon Andrew's hand covered hers again. His eyes were filled with warmth, offering respite that was too hard to resist. She clutched his hand so tightly it had to have hurt. But she couldn't let him go.

"You're so strong, Serena. You thought you had to be for so long. But you don't have to be."

She loosened her grasp in small increments, staring out the window into the illuminated parking lot. If only his words could overcome the resistance deep within her.

"But Tessa needs me. I have to be strong for her. I'm all she has."

He slipped his hand away, bending and straightening his fingers a few times after her tight grip. "Yes, Tessa does need you, but more than that, she needs to know where you're getting your strength from. Don't you think it's about time that you let go and let God heal your broken heart?"

Serena wrapped her hands around her coffee cup, needing something to do. "I'm trying. It's just so hard."

"In the Book of Matthew, Jesus said, 'Come to

me, all who labor and are heavy laden, and I will give you rest.' You don't have to carry all of your burdens alone.'' He stopped and stared into her eyes. ''If you're honest with yourself, you'll realize you haven't been doing it alone, anyway. The Father has been carrying you all along—at least, as far as you would allow Him to.''

It all made sense. Sometimes she would reach the end of a particularly grueling day and wonder how she'd survived the blur of events. And somehow, the next day she'd get up and do it all over again. ''Rest. That sounds good. I feel like I've been on a top that's been spinning so long it's wobbling and threatening to topple.''

''So, fall. It's okay. He'll catch you. And I'll be there, too, if that makes any difference.''

''It makes a difference.'' Their gazes connected again and held in a link that felt stronger than ever before. When she finally looked away, Serena felt as warm as if he'd held her in his arms. If only she could trust the Father to do the same.

''Do you think you're ready to let go and allow God to take control?''

She wanted to say yes so badly that the word burned on her tongue. It was what Andrew wanted to hear. But was she ready to open her hands and let go completely? She wasn't sure. And she couldn't bear to lie to Andrew, or to God. When she committed herself, it would be for keeps. She had to be prepared not to yank the reins of control when she faced her darkest moments. She wasn't quite there.

"I will be soon." She hoped with all her soul that she spoke the truth.

Serena walked several paces ahead of Andrew on the sidewalk, her dark hair shimmering in the street lamp's yellow glow. This wasn't what he'd had in mind when suggesting a walk after their motorcycle ride back to Serena's. He'd hoped for hand-holding and more closeness than this.

"Do you think Hannah looked like she'd been crying?" she asked over her shoulder.

"I don't know. Maybe." He didn't want to talk about troubled teens or injections or anything that involved anyone other than the two of them. Just this once, he wanted Serena all to himself, if only for the time it took to walk around the block.

But his own worry crowded his best attempt at being selfish. Hannah hadn't looked right at all when they'd stopped by the house, before setting out on foot. He stopped walking.

"Yes, she'd been crying."

Serena turned toward him. "What should we do?"

"I'm not sure. She's always been a sad girl, the whole time I've known her. She's never fully recovered from her mother's death."

She stopped, as well, glancing toward a two-story house that was dark except for a single upstairs light. "Would any child completely recover from that? I wonder what made tonight especially bad. Could it be the anniversary?''

"I don't think so. I think Reverend Bob said his wife died at Christmastime.''

Serena started walking again, forcing Andrew to jog to catch up. "Then, maybe it's something else. You don't think it's about a boy, do you?''

"I've never seen her with a boyfriend." As soon as the words were out of his mouth, Andrew knew that probably wasn't true. Either there was something between Hannah and Todd, or one of them wished there were. Still, that didn't mean she wasn't crying about her mom.

"I'll ask her about it on the way home," he promised. "Now, can we just walk?''

He playfully elbowed her, but instead of returning his jab, Serena leaned in to him. He gave thanks for his skin's strength as it was the only thing that kept his insides from leaping out every which way.

The need to be close to her, to touch her, was palpable, but he weighed his decision before taking her hand. She responded in the best way he could have hoped for—lacing her fingers through his in a connection so perfect that their hands must have been created for that purpose.

Something had changed between them. He'd tried to convince himself that he'd imagined her arms tightening around him on the ride home. He smiled into the darkness over being wrong.

Her hand felt so delicate in his, such a contrast from those of the powerhouse of a woman who'd taken on the world for her child's sake. But this was the side of her he'd longed to see, the part that appealed to his need to protect, to cherish. They walked on in silence, the only sounds coming from crickets that refused to quiet their tunes.

She didn't seem to need conversation any more than he did. Just being together was enough. He couldn't imagine any place he'd rather be, any person who could inspire in him a more intense need for connection, for a melding of hands and hearts. For keeps.

He smoothed his thumb over the back of her hand. Had he felt her trembling? Was it anything like the way he shook with the need to be near her, the desire to make their relationship more significant than friendship?

When they reached the other side of the block from Serena's house, Andrew stopped under a street lamp and faced her. Their hands remained loosely linked. "Serena, we need to talk."

She chewed her lip. "I know we do."

"I want to be more than your friend."

She shook her head, but her hand quivered again within his. "I just don't know what is right. I shouldn't—"

He couldn't let her finish, not when her words might dash his only chance at happiness. Lifting her hand, he pressed his lips to her knuckles. "I'd love to kiss you, but I want to know that it means as much to you as it does to me. Would you like me to kiss you, Serena?"

He waited for her answer, still hearing the musical ring her spoken name left in his ears. She shook all over. As much as he longed to draw her into his arms and chase away her fears, he couldn't. His wanting them to be together wasn't enough to change her heart. The choice had to be hers, even if his battered heart hung exposed.

"Yes," she whispered.

If he hadn't been straining his ears against the silence, he wouldn't have heard her at all. What felt like the most precious gift settled around him in a fine mist as he moved his hands to her waist and pulled her to him.

He touched his lips to hers just once and pulled away, his skin still yearning for that exquisite touch. Then she slipped her hands around his neck and drew him back down to her. Her sweet kiss felt like a promise made…a promise kept. And he couldn't have felt less worthy.

Shaken, Andrew cradled her in his arms, slanting his mouth over hers and deepening the kiss. This was his own commitment, one that terrified him almost as much as it thrilled him. It pledged qualities he wasn't sure he possessed, bespoke a magical future he couldn't possibly know. He prayed it was a promise he could keep.

Chapter Twelve

She had to be glowing. Serena stepped to the front door, tamping down that golden light within her. She longed to clasp Andrew's hand in hers, to never let go—even in front of Hannah—but she couldn't allow herself to cling. Their relationship was too new. Too fragile.

"Hannah, we're back," she called before she was fully through the front door.

Hannah jerked up on the couch as if she'd been caught doing something terrible and turned her head away to wipe her swollen eyes. She stood and smiled weakly, but misery hovered over her.

It didn't seem right to be this happy when Hannah's world was so dark. The mother in Serena awakened, making her long to rock the child in her arms. She glanced at Andrew, who nodded at her unspoken message.

He moved to the stairs. "I'm going to go check on Tessa."

Hannah hopped up from the couch. "I'd better put those popcorn bowls in the dishwasher."

"Don't worry about that." Serena sat on the arm of the sofa and patted a spot for the teenager to sit. "Something is upsetting you. Is there anything I can do?"

"It's nothing...really." She wiped her eyes and rubbed the wetness on her white shorts.

"Most people don't cry about 'nothing.'"

Hannah shifted on the couch and licked her lips. "Well...you know my mother died. I guess I'm just missing her more than usual today. It's hard being a teen without a mom. Dad tries, but you know how guys are. He just doesn't get it."

It all sounded plausible, almost too believable. Her explanation was too easily placed in a box and tied up with a red ribbon. That was why Serena didn't buy it. Everything Hannah had said was probably true—except that it wasn't the reason she'd been crying.

Serena's thoughts leaped back to the theory about teenage turmoil over a boy. Could it be Todd? There was certainly more to Hannah and her "friend" than she'd been telling. How could Serena get her to confide in her so she could help?

After five minutes of silence in the living room, Andrew returned, lifting an eyebrow at Serena. She shook her head.

He placed a hand on Serena's shoulder. "Hannah, Serena and I have decided to start dating."

Hannah almost smiled. "So you've finally decided to make it official." Her candor was startling. "You two are about as transparent as cellophane. Everyone can see that you belong together."

Andrew cleared his throat. "What I was trying to say was that Tessa will need a semi-regular babysitter, if you're up for the job."

She shrugged. "Okay, I guess."

Hannah stood and nervously tidied up even though there was no longer any clutter. Why was it so easy for a teenager to accept Andrew and Serena as a couple when Serena had been hiding from the reality? She looked up in time to see Andrew staring down at her. And she couldn't stop looking back at the man who was excavating the stone wall around her heart.

"See what I mean?" Hannah's words broke the trance. "I'll wait outside."

Andrew pulled Serena to her feet and into his arms in one smooth move. He lowered his head for a single, gentle kiss. But when they pulled away, both looked toward the screen door Hannah had closed behind her.

Concern for the teenager clouded Serena's joy. "How can we help her?" She glanced out the window again. Hannah stood at the curb under the street lamp, looking as if she were alone in the world. "She needs us."

Andrew shrugged, his brow furrowing. "Although Reverend Bob has asked me to try to reach his daughter, until now, she's not given me much opportunity. Maybe this is it. Maybe having her baby-sit for Tessa will make her comfortable enough to open up to us. We need to be there for her when she's ready.''

He faced Serena again, slipping his fingers through her hair. Then he closed his arms around her.

She relished the warmth of his hug for a few seconds before pulling away. "That was your only reason for suggesting she be my baby-sitter?" She grinned at him. "It was pure unselfishness?"

"What can I say? I'm a selfless guy."

She felt his kiss—not a simple peck, but a caress with the pressure of permanence. It felt more like a connection of hearts than lips, as if his arteries had taken over supplying lifeblood to her while her veins were busy returning that valuable supply to him. How could she have been reluctant to accept the gift of being this close to Andrew Westin? She'd needed a connection with him more than she ever could have imagined.

He kissed the tip of her nose. "I'm going to be very selfish with you."

Selfish. Serena thought about that word two weeks later and was amazed at how true—and false—it had turned out to be. Yes, Andrew had been selfish with her attention, but only when they were having a quiet dinner or walking along the paths at Kensington Metropark.

At church, he'd given her a wide berth, not making their personal relationship a public issue, although the congregation was aware of it, courtesy of Charity. Hannah had kept pretty quiet about the arrangement.

Selfish. There was no way he could have been described that way during their times with Tessa. Serena ticked off a list of their adventures lately, amazed they'd done all of that and still had time for just the two of them.

The three of them had been to the beach, Central Park and the "mountain top playground" built over the old landfill in South Lyon, and out for pizza. Andrew had been far too indulgent with beautiful children's books at Read Between the Lines bookstore downtown. And, as always, he'd been right there on Wednesdays, offering a pair of securing hands for Tessa's shot, which was already becoming much less of a struggle.

Serena brushed her hair before the mirror and clipped it in a ponytail. Next she applied mascara and lipstick. Even if tonight was a ruse, she wanted to dress the part. Looking nice for Andrew was important to her, although he preferred her with no makeup and with helmet-head hair after a motorcycle ride. What did he know, anyway?

As well as keeping her and her daughter thoroughly entertained the past two weeks, Andrew had also done everything but stand on his head and sing

"The Battle Hymn of the Republic" to get Hannah to tell them what was troubling her. Serena guessed he might try even that, if their plan failed tonight.

To her credit, Hannah had kept her feelings locked up tighter than a bank vault. She'd even begun putting on a happy face when she came over, but that had only raised more red flags. Serena couldn't shake the feeling that Hannah might be contemplating suicide, and that she and Andrew might be the girl's only lifeline. Tonight's "intervention" had been born out of that worry.

Ready too early, she paced in the living room. Maybe this was all a mistake. They probably should have talked to Reverend Bob about their concern for his daughter. But what would they have told him? That Hannah seemed sad? It was too late to worry now.

Serena heard the roar of the Harley coming up the street.

"Mommy, Mr. Andrew's here!" Tessa ran down the stairs, a beanbag cat tucked under each arm. She watched out the window as Andrew parked. "You didn't say Hannah was coming."

"That's the fun part, punky. Hannah is baby-sitting *me* tonight. You're going on an adventure with Mr. Andrew."

Tessa dropped her toys, planting her hands on her hips and rolling her eyes. "Silly Mommy. You're big. You don't need a baby-sitter."

"Okay, you caught me. I just want to spend a little time with Hannah. Is that okay with you?"

Tessa pressed her index finger to her lips, seeming to ponder before nodding.

Outside, the two stepped off the motorcycle, removing their helmets. Serena prayed for guidance. It felt good to concentrate on someone else's problems, working as a team with Andrew to reach out to Hannah.

Andrew jogged up the walk, his hair all messed from his helmet. Just watching him, Serena felt her heart flutter, forcing her to admit that her anticipation for tonight had to do with more than their plan. It was the same feeling that filtered through her whenever he was near her, whenever he played with Tessa, whenever he telephoned her—even when she *thought* about him calling her.

As he stepped on the porch, coming nearer, Serena saw the words that had been dancing on the periphery of her consciousness for days line up before her eyes like skywriting. *I love you.* Not just *like,* but *love.* The realization was frightening, but the feeling itself was wonderful, and, quite possibly, heaven-sent.

Hannah looked back and forth between the two adults incredulously. "What do you mean you don't need me to baby-sit?" She looked even worse than she had two days before, the blueing crescents beneath her eyes more visible.

Serena placed a hand under her elbow, leading her into the room. "I thought you and I could use some time to get to know each other better."

Tessa was already in Andrew's arms. "My mommy said you were going to baby-sit *her* tonight."

"I don't think she needs a baby-sitter." Hannah stuffed her hands in her shorts pockets, appearing more angry than nervous.

Tessa shrugged. "That's what I told her."

Andrew cleared his throat. "Well, Tess and I have an adventure to go on, so we're out of here."

"Mommy, do I get to ride the motorcycle?"

"Hold it right there." Serena held up one hand in a sign to stop, while still facing the angry teenager, who looked as if she might bolt. "You'll take my car." With her free hand, she fished the keys from her pocket and tossed them to Andrew.

"You're not leaving me here, are you?" For the first time, Hannah looked frightened.

Andrew patted her shoulder. "We'll be back soon." He scooted out the door and waved from the driveway.

Serena turned back to Hannah. The teen's words rushed at her so quickly, she didn't have time to worry about where to begin.

"Why do you two keep hounding me?" Hannah folded her arms over her chest. "There's nothing wrong with me. I need to call my father and have him come get me."

Hannah reached for the phone, but Serena covered the receiver with her hand. "What will you tell him? That those dark circles under your eyes and those ribs that have to be showing through your skin are the same 'nothing' that you've been telling me about for the past two weeks?''

"It's none of your business." Hannah shook her head, fighting a battle with tears and losing. "It's nobody's business."

Serena drew her over to sit on the sofa. "But you need to tell someone, Hannah. I'll listen. I'll help you if you want me to, but most of all, I'll listen."

"I don't need your help. I'm fine. Why won't you believe me?"

She pulled Hannah into her arms and, despite the girl's initial resistance, held her. "Because you look like you've just lost your best friend."

Hannah sobbed into Serena's shirtfront. "I did."

Serena pulled her away so she could look in her eyes. "What do you mean?"

"Todd's dad got transferred to Singapore. He left two weeks ago."

Serena sensed there was more to this story, just as she'd felt that there was more to the relationship between Hannah and her friend. "I'm sorry to hear that."

"Have you ever had a best friend?"

Andrew's face entered Serena's mind with startling accuracy. How strange it was that if she'd been asked that question a few months before, she'd have said no. But her life was different now. "Yes, I have one. I understand how sad you must feel that Todd is gone, but you can always stay in contact."

"It's not like he was my boyfriend or anything."

"Of course, just a special friend."

The temptation was great to suggest that, like herself, Hannah might have been in love with her best friend. Serena resisted. They'd come too far in this conversation for her to send it rolling back to "there's nothing wrong." Anyway, maybe her love was the something extra Hannah wasn't telling.

"When I'm feeling down, I always do something that makes me feel wonderful. Eat ice cream," said Serena.

She led Hannah into the kitchen and opened the freezer. After twenty minutes of fancy creating, they settled back onto the couch, sitting cross-legged and balancing bowls of vanilla ice cream, chocolate syrup and sprinkles on their laps. They were licking their spoons and laughing together by the time Andrew flipped open the front door, with Tessa planted on his shoulders.

"Boy, did we have a wonderful adventure, checking out the fish in the water and watching those illegal people feeding bread to the geese in the park."

Tessa examined their empty bowls. "We had fun, but we didn't get ice cream."

Andrew couldn't think of a sound that made him feel better than the tinkling-of-ice-cubes that was Serena's laugh. And she'd somehow managed to make the saddest young girl he knew laugh, as well. It was amazing the healing that Serena brought to people's lives.

Just look at how she'd affected his life. A heart that had been dead was beating powerfully in his chest, so alive in its new capacity for emotion. Serena was responsible for that.

He grinned as he entered the room, watching her profile as she shared some girlfriend joke with Hannah. Just when had he fallen in love with her? He had no idea of time or place, but the feeling was there as clear as a crystal box, with just as much potential to be opened and filled with more wonder.

Could his heart have been lost that first day when she'd come into his office, searching for answers? Or was it the day at the beach when she'd intrigued him with her thoughts, charmed him with the sweet way she mothered her child, entranced him with her beauty—inside and out? Or had it happened as gradually as a spring thaw, the ice melting from his heart in a slow, steady trickle?

No matter how he'd arrived, he was here now, in the only place he wanted to be. A single day of loving Serena was far better than a lifetime of "safe" loneliness.

She looked up at him then, a tiny droplet of chocolate syrup stuck on the corner of her mouth, until she wiped it away with her thumb. He wanted to tell her how he felt. He wanted to announce it from the pulpit.

But, no, he was getting ahead of himself. Serena was only a fraction less fragile than the willowy teenager giggling beside her on the couch. What if his feelings, so powerful that they overwhelmed even him, sent her running in another direction? He could already anticipate the corresponding implosion of his heart.

Fear welled within, where warmth had settled so lightly only moments before. Loving Serena—or at least letting her know how he felt—suddenly seemed like the most dangerous thing in the world. She'd tried to convince him that not only God but also His creation had the capacity for good. He was beginning to believe she was right, but he wasn't ready for a test.

He couldn't tell her. Not yet. Not until he was sure she felt the same. Would he ever be able to trust that far, to place his happiness and future in her hands? Could he have the faith to practice what he preached?

Until Tessa tapped him on the head, Andrew didn't realize he'd been staring or how long he'd stood there, looking foolish. Both Serena and Hannah were watching him, mirth pulling at the corners of their mouths.

"Mr. Andrew, put me down. I want some ice cream." As soon as her feet touched the floor, Tessa raced off toward the kitchen.

"Me, too," he chimed, following her toward the freezer. Maybe ice cream would do him some good. He sure needed something to cool off his thoughts.

"Are you going to tell me what Hannah said or not?" Andrew tapped the phone's receiver impatiently.

"I'll tell you, but I'm pretty sure what she told

me wasn't the whole story.'' She hesitated, wondering why she was suddenly uncomfortable retelling Hannah's story to even Andrew. Her motherly protective urge was kicking in. Still, Andrew was just as concerned for Hannah as she was, and had as much right to know. ''Her best friend, Todd, moved far away, and she feels lost.''

''I can see how hard that would be.'' He paused for several seconds. ''Especially when she's in love with him.''

It was strange how it didn't feel as if they were talking about two teenage sweethearts at all, but two adult ones who were more best friends and soul mates than these two adolescents could ever be.

''I think I know what that must be like.'' Serena swallowed hard.

Panic burst through her so quickly that her ears pounded. What had she done? She'd all but admitted she was in love with him, and he'd said nothing. Silence hung on the line between them until she wanted to scream. How dare he let her hang there in this interminable quiet, after she'd opened up to him! He owed her more than that—at least a subject change.

''Serena…you and I…together, we…''

She couldn't stand it anymore, listening to him struggle through the most awkward letdown known to man or woman. He was a youth minister, trained as public speaker, and he couldn't find the words to make this horrible moment pass. To let her down easily.

"Of course, Andrew, *together we* can help Hannah face her sadness. We make a great team working with the youth." Each word was a new brick mortared into her path of loneliness.

The humiliation was unbearable. Images of Trent and his new wife flashed before her eyes. How naive she'd been to believe that Trent's infidelity was the most pain a person could endure in a lifetime. It was like a pothole next to the Grand Canyon of her heartache over Andrew. It stretched before her eyes like a fuchsia haze. Andrew had embedded himself deeply in her heart, and now his rejection had carved the center out.

"No, Serena, that's not what I meant. What I meant—"

A pounding, loud enough for even Andrew to have heard it through the phone line, sounded at the door. It cut off what could only have been a more awkward attempt to end the call. Relieved, Serena carried the phone with her to the door and opened it to a sobbing Hannah, who fell like a heap into her arms.

"Serena, what is it?" Andrew called into the line.

"I have to go. I'll call you later."

As she pulled the handset away from her face to turn off the "talk" button, she heard his fading words. "I'll be right there."

Chapter Thirteen

"It's going to be just fine." Serena sat on the sofa beside Hannah, pulling her into her arms. Glancing up the stairs to see if all the clatter had awakened her own child, she mourned for this girl whose mother had left her for heaven. She hoped that if ever Tessa were alone, she would find a pair of arms to hold her, too.

She rubbed soothing circles over Hannah's back, as the girl's sobs shook them both. It seemed hours before the wails were reduced to whimpers. Only then did Serena pull Hannah away from her own wet robe, so she could meet her gaze.

"It's time, Hannah. Tell me the secret that's killing you."

"I'm pregnant."

Her suspicion confirmed, Serena's heart pounded as she lived out any parent's nightmare with another's child. "Are you sure?"

Hannah nodded, a residual sob ripping from her lungs.

"Can you tell me who the baby's father is?"

She shook her head hard. "No. It's nobody you know."

Serena didn't believe that for a minute, but it was pointless to argue. Relief filled her as another, softer knock came at the door. Her other feelings were so easy to compartmentalize right now, when Hannah's tragedy had to be the most important thing. Andrew was there to help, and she needed him as much as Hannah did.

When Andrew stepped in the door, Hannah looked prepared to leap from the couch and run, but he slowly approached her, then sat and gathered her into his arms. "Hannah, let me help."

This was the man whom Serena had fallen in love with. If he never came to the place in his life when he could return her feelings, she'd still remember this as the moment when she loved him most of all.

"Can you tell me what it is?" Andrew asked softly, patting her back in a steady rhythm. Hannah shook her head, but nodded when he asked if Serena could tell him.

He sat quietly, taking it all in, no sign of judgment in his expression, only the compassion of a true minister.

Andrew spoke softly to Hannah. "Have you told Todd?"

"No…" She stumbled over the word. "What do you mean?"

"Have you told him he's going to be a father?"

"No, no. It's not Todd. It's somebody else."

Hannah sobbed again. Maybe Andrew wasn't handling the situation so well after all.

"Hannah says the father is someone we don't know. And that Todd is only a friend."

Andrew nodded. "Well, none of that is as important as helping you and your unborn child. I take it you haven't told your dad yet."

Another wave of tears followed. When they subsided, he pulled her away from his chest again. "You know you have to tell him, and soon. You can't hide this for long."

She nodded, burying her face in her hands.

He brushed the hair, matted to her cheek with tears, back behind her ears and let her lean against his shoulder. "Rest now. Everything will look clearer in the morning."

Serena drew a quilt off the back of the couch, tucked it around Hannah's shoulders and sat on the opposite side of the girl so they could comfort her between them. The next few hours were a blur of sobs and silence, weeping and recovery, until Hannah finally found the peace of sleep with her head in Serena's lap.

Andrew came through the front door early the next morning, crossed to the kitchen and laid Serena's keys on the table beside her. "Well, I got her home."

"Did she make it inside okay?"

"It looked like it." He lowered himself into the kitchen chair with an exhausted plop. Sitting across the table from him, Serena looked about as bleary-eyed as he felt. He guzzled from the mug of coffee she poured for him. The liquid settled inside him like a lead ball, but he drank it, anyway. Something had to clear his vision.

Already he questioned their decision to help Hannah sneak back into the house so she could have a few days to gather courage to face her father. Reverend Bob was his friend. Andrew had no right to deceive him, even if his motive was good.

"She's going to be okay, you know."

Serena seemed convinced of her words. He only hoped she was right. He reached for her hand and prayed. "Lord, please give Hannah strength as she faces one of the most difficult periods in her life. Give her Your peace and guidance as she decides the direction for herself and her unborn child. Amen."

Squeezing her hand once more, he released it, feeling an immediate sense of loss in the disconnection. He was glad Tessa hadn't awakened as he walked to the door, with Serena a few steps behind him. Making explanations for something so innocent would lend an element of indecency that had been absent last night.

He stared back at her, smiling the kiss and hug he would have given her if he weren't too tired, his mind too weary. He needed to hold her and be held by her, to be filled by the comfort only she could give.

In his first clear thought of the day, he remembered her words on the telephone last night. *I think I know what it must be like.* Had she been telling him she loved him? That had to be it.

And when he could have given a perfect response to her precious words, all he did was trip over his tongue. Why couldn't he just tell her the truth—that he loved her more than he ever could have imagined? Later, after they'd both rested, he'd tell her everything.

He stepped out the door and felt all of his plans drift slowly away. "This day is going to be a long one." The shiny Lincoln, parked next to his Harley, would have looked out of place in this neighborhood, even if Charity weren't leaning against it with her arms crossed.

"Well, this is a disappointing turn of events." The smug look on her face didn't reflect any of her "disappointment."

Andrew glanced back at Serena, looking mortified in the doorway as she tightened her robe over her lounging pajamas. *Incriminating* was too weak a word to describe how this looked.

"Good morning, Charity."

"I don't see how you can act so casually when you've just been found to be in sin with this...woman."

Serena stepped out the door, nervously messing

with the collar of her robe. ''It's not what you think, Charity. Once Andrew tells—''

Andrew stopped her by resolutely shaking his head. What had to be shock and pain registered in her eyes.

''What do you have to say for yourself, youth minister Andrew?'' Charity planted her hands on her hips. ''How do you plan to explain this away? What do you suggest I do now, teacher?''

She came dangerously close to grinning. He pitied her for having to see someone else's pain to feed her need for superiority. ''Please, Charity, just wait a few days. The truth will come to light, and everything will be explained.''

She shook her head, walking up to face him. ''There's no way I'd give you two the opportunity to come up with more lies than the ones you've already been living before the congregation and before God.''

He nodded, feeling empty, helpless. ''Then, do what you have to do.''

She marched toward her car and spoke over her shoulder. ''You bet I will.'' She got in and sped away.

Andrew stomped toward his motorcycle with every bit of anger he'd felt all his life carrying him in its force. As he pulled away from the curb, he watched Serena rush into her house.

A better man would have returned to comfort her. A better man wouldn't have hurt her in the first place. Obviously, he wasn't that man, even if his reasons were defendable. It had been a self-fulfilling prophesy that he'd hurt the woman he loved.

Nobility in Hannah's defense was exacting a huge price for him personally, and possibly a bigger one from Serena. When it was all over, could she ever forgive him?

Betrayed. Serena knew she shouldn't feel that way, but she did. Andrew had only done what he'd felt was right to protect Hannah's privacy. It was probably even his job to ensure the girl's confidentiality. But all of this was happening at her expense.

They'd been accused of having an affair and, rather than defend her, Andrew had sacrificed her to Charity's revenge. She wanted to be forgiving. But all she could be was furious.

Charity had been like a piranha, swimming in to devour exposed flesh. It had taken all of Serena's strength to keep from slapping that self-satisfied look off the other woman's face. But why was she wasting her anger on Charity, who was only being her sanctimonious Pharisee self? Andrew was the true culprit here.

It was so obvious now that he didn't love her. That amazing way he'd looked at her—as if she'd filled some empty place in the center of his soul— had been a product of her imagination. If he cared about her, he would have protected her reputation, her dignity, whatever his personal cost. He'd never have sacrificed her, no matter how noble the reason.

His betrayal covered her hope in darkness. The

knowledge that she'd have to go forward without his love only deepened the night, giving no promise of morning.

Why had she been such a fool as to trust him with her heart? She should have known better, but she couldn't help it when she saw what seemed to be his pure faith in her. So she'd released control. Look where it had gotten her.

She folded the quilt on the sofa and picked up a few empty pop cans from last night. All she had to do was make it into her room and inside her closet to that tiny secret room in the back. Tears would be okay there, if she could make it that far.

But her vision clouded as she climbed the stairs. Tessa met her at the top.

"Hi, Mommy. Why are you crying?"

Serena wiped the dampness into the shoulder of her robe. "I'm fine. Did you have a nice sleep?"

"Yep. Can we have pancakes?"

Serena pasted on her best smile. "Absolutely."

In fact, if someone could overdose on mother-daughter activities, she and Tessa would do it that day. She was fine. And they'd be fine together. Just the two of them. That was the way it was supposed to be. The way it had to be, no matter how much she wished it otherwise.

"Then we can go to the beach. And maybe later we'll get ice cream. How does that sound?"

Tessa's squeal was enough of an answer.

Serena was grateful for the numbness that settled inside her while she flipped pancakes and chiseled the dried batter off the counter where Tessa had poured a few silver-dollar ones. Moping would have to wait, because their day wouldn't.

"Mommy, where's your swimsuit?" Tessa came through the doorway, sporting a teddy bear one-piece and flip-flops and tugging along her bags of sand toys.

"Give me five minutes." Serena mounted the stairs, unbuttoning her pajamas. The need to hurry pressed her forward like a hand from behind. She had to keep moving, keep having fun with her daughter. It didn't matter how tired she was from the night of helping Hannah. If she slowed down, she'd have time to think, time to feel. That was unacceptable.

That would mean having to think about how quickly word of their alleged affair would filter through the congregation. It would mean pondering whether she should find another church—or another town. And it would mean seeing Andrew's face and wishing things were different.

No, she couldn't do this. It would only bring more tears. Useless tears that wouldn't make any difference. She wiggled into her swimsuit and wrestled her hair into a messy bun, focusing on beach umbrellas, multicolored beach towels, sand buckets and shovels.

"Hurry up, Mommy," Tessa yelled up the stairs. "Are we ever going to the beach?"

Serena pulled a hooded cover-up over her head,

grabbed her beach bag and headed downstairs. "Sure we are. We're going right now."

They'd carried their "necessities" to the car and Serena had buckled Tessa into her car seat, when Tessa realized she'd left her inflatable duck float in the house.

Serena jogged back up the steps and unlocked the door in time to hear the phone ring. As much as she wanted to let it go to the machine, she thought about her possibly dwindling freelance base.

That sounded better than admitting she couldn't stand not knowing if it was Andrew. She grabbed the portable handset and jogged out to open the car door so Tessa wouldn't melt.

"Hello?"

"Serena…it's Trent."

She gasped. Why now? Why couldn't this have happened when she was stronger? Why not when she could have found the right words?

"What is it, Trent?"

"We need to talk."

"I think it's all been said. I can't imagine anything else we can say."

"I read the report the hospital sent to Tessa's pediatrician. They sent me a copy because she's still on my insurance. It sounds like she is doing well, growing even."

Panic ticked inside her, a time bomb without the cushion of at least an hour or two before detonation. "So?"

"So I want to see Tessa's improvement for myself."

*   *   *

Andrew was amazed at how quickly a deacons'
meeting could be called when the youth minister
was accused of impropriety. Just a matter of hours.
Who was he kidding? If he weren't the accused, he,
too, would have expected swift action by the
church's governing board, as well.

Still, he couldn't help feeling like a catfish invited
to a fish fry. After making it through the whole
morning—through hospital visits and a meeting with
leaders from the ecumenical food pantry—he dared
to believe that Charity had for once been charitable
and given him a few days' reprieve to clear his
name. Their names. But when Reverend Bob peeked
inside his door, Andrew knew it had been wishful
thinking.

"Son, may I come in?"

In the entire time he'd been at the church, Andrew
couldn't remember Reverend Bob, twenty-five years
his senior, ever calling him "son." It felt too con-
descending. But when the minister walked in and
sat in the visitor's chair opposite Andrew's desk, it
was clear the minister wasn't trying to take a power
position with him. Even his face bore the same compassionate, nonjudgmental expression he shared
with all of the sinners on Sundays.

"I take it we have some talking to do," Reverend
Bob said.

How strange it was to see the minister in the same
chair where Andrew had seen Serena up close for

the first time, where he'd first felt drawn to her. Would she look back on the moment when she'd walked into his life with anything but regret?

He could never see it that way. Every step they'd taken together since that first meeting, every word they'd spoken, had drawn him closer to this point. This was where he'd choose to be the man God had created him to be by standing up for what he knew was right. He owed Serena so much for helping him get there. He loved her even more.

"I guess we do." Andrew watched his friend, ready to reach out to him in his time of need. Reverend Bob would need friends just as badly when the truth came out.

The minister cleared his throat uncomfortably. "Charity Sims has accused you and Mrs. Jacobs of sin. It would take a blind person not to see the way you two look at each other. Not to see that you're in love. But it appears obvious that you need to be married…right away."

Andrew rested his elbows on the desk and leaned into his hands. "I agree with almost everything you've said. I want to marry Serena—the sooner, the better. But it's not about sin. Serena has done nothing wrong, except caring for me, trusting me."

"I'm not sure I understand. Charity said she saw you coming out of Serena's home this morning, looking as if you'd been there all night."

Andrew pushed past the need to strike back, to toss his resentment toward Charity at Reverend Bob because he was a convenient target. He looked directly at the older man. "You and I have become good friends. If I told you that you had only to wait a few days, and the truth would come out, would you trust me?"

"Of course, I'd trust you. I'm not here to judge you. Only our Lord has that right."

Doing the right thing could be a lonely job. It was such a relief to know that he wouldn't have to face his mission alone. "You'll see. Just as Jesus told His followers that they would know the truth and be made free by it, I promise you that the truth in this situation will be freeing to all of us."

Reverend Bob stood and planted his palms on the desk. "Why don't you just tell me? If I know the truth, I'm sure we'll be able to work this out."

"I can't." *It's not my place.* Hannah deserved the opportunity to tell her father. He had to give her a chance. "I can only ask you to trust me and wait."

The minister dropped back in the chair as if the wind had just been ripped from his sails. He stared at the floor a long time before finally lifting his head.

"I'll do both of those things for you, my friend. Trust and wait." Reverend Bob folded his hands together in a prayerful pose. "But I'm afraid I can't protect you. My believing in you won't be enough to prevent the deacons from searching for the truth—in their time, not yours. And it won't stop them from taking whatever action they believe is necessary."

Andrew nodded. His heart felt heavy despite his

certainty that he'd made the right decision. The price seemed higher than he would have guessed. No one this side of heaven could protect him now, just as he was unable to shield Serena from the humiliation he'd subjected her to.

Only his Lord could make a difference. He who had the ability to show sunsets to the blind, introduce marathon running to the lame, repair all the pieces of a fractured heart needed to do only one small thing this time.

Please, Andrew prayed, *lead Hannah to do the right thing.*

Chapter Fourteen

Serena jogged up the walk, balancing a picnic basket on one hip and a beach umbrella under the opposite arm. If only she had enough hands to juggle the clash of issues that just wouldn't leave her alone.

"Mommy," Tessa wailed from the open car door, her five-minute nap having ended at the curb.

"I'll be right back, honey," Serena called back, propping the picnic basket and beach umbrella on her hip while wrestling with the front-door lock.

"Mommy, carry me."

Before the entire neighborhood begged her to take the child inside, Serena dumped her first load by the door and rushed back to the car. She carried Tessa to bed, feeling the child's weight go heavy as she drifted back to sleep.

Hopelessness settled around Serena again as soon as she closed her daughter's bedroom door. Even the sun, the sand and the water—with Tessa frolicking in the center of it all—hadn't been enough to extricate this madness from her mind. What kind of mother was she that she couldn't lose herself in her daughter's squeals of joy?

Instead, she'd focused on her own misery. And now that misery went beyond losing the love of her life. Trent had rolled back in and made himself a part of the mess. How dare he call now, when Tessa was doing better! Where had he been when her skin was burning with fevers or when her joints doubled in size?

No, Serena wasn't about to let Trent weasel his way back into her daughter's life now. It didn't matter that, out of the blue, Tessa had started asking when they'd go see Daddy. Or that her drawings had begun to include a small stick person surrounded by three big stick people—Tessa with Serena, Andrew and Trent. She couldn't put her child's heart in jeopardy again.

Tessa was healthy today, but what about tomorrow? When her illness flared again, when she struggled to run across the front yard or do such simple tasks as brushing her teeth, her father would be looking for another parachute. Serena would make sure he never even boarded that plane.

Keeping busy now, she unpacked their wet and sandy beach things. But she couldn't move faster than the thoughts that hounded her, devouring what little hope she had left.

The worst part was knowing that if Trent pushed the issue, he could get visitation whether she liked it or not. The court had granted him that even in the divorce settlement. He'd paid child support regularly, but he'd not shown any interest in exercising his right to see his own child. Until now.

Under attack, Serena wished she could protect her daughter from inside some safe zone. She used to think Andrew was part of that protected place, but she couldn't have been more wrong.

She was in no mental state to settle her life's problems today. Instead, she'd make the only kind of decisions she could handle right now—those between serif and sans serif fonts and bold and italic text in the new tri-fold brochure for the area builders' association.

She sat at her computer and focused on the screen. At least the consequences of these decisions weren't as critical as the others plaguing her mind. If the product stunk when she printed it out, she could always change it. She wished she had that latitude in other areas.

Reading her last paragraph of lousy text, she massaged her temples. This job had suddenly become more critical. She couldn't afford to put out substandard work, especially now. Milford was a small town. Before long, her personal embarrassment would become break-room fodder at Kroger's. Would businesses trust her with their promotional materials after she'd been branded an immoral person?

Either way, the work would be more critical in the next few months. It would need to be superb. So these extraneous thoughts sneaking into her head just had to go.

She spent the next hour singularly focused on the computer screen and keyboard. It felt good to complete a task instead of wasting energy on something she couldn't change. Creativity, so elusive until now, began to flow steadily. Everything would be fine. She'd survive it all—even this new threat with Trent—on her own. The way she'd survived everything else.

The phone rang, interrupting her thoughts.

"Serena, it's Andrew."

As if she wouldn't have recognized that voice even if she were blindfolded at a district-wide Christian men's breakfast. She tried to mentally slow her racing heart. She wanted to give him the verbal smack he deserved, but there was no forcing even a whistle past her constricted vocal cords. So she let the silence speak for her.

"Before you hang up, please let me explain."

She got her voice back then. "Like you explained to Charity?"

"I deserve that. But I want to apologize."

She closed her eyes against the pain. She needed to at least listen to him and try to understand. "You did what you had to do."

"I did. But I'm still sorry I hurt you by doing it."

"Thanks for saying so." It was the best she could do. She was glad that he'd at least acknowledged his decision had affected her, but his apology didn't change things.

An uncomfortable silence hung on the line until he finally cracked it. "I'm at the church. There's an emergency deacons' meeting in an hour."

Serena forgot all pretense of being aloof. This call wasn't about her humiliation. It wasn't about her at all—not if she really listened to his unspoken plea for support. The man she loved was about to be fired for doing what was right. Where was the justice in that?

"She didn't waste any time, did she."

"Charity did what she felt she had to do."

She did what hurt the most. Had he forgiven Charity? That didn't seem possible, when all Serena wanted do was scratch the woman's eyes out. But he didn't need her vengeful thoughts now. "I'm glad you've mastered the art of forgiveness."

"I haven't *mastered* anything. This is all brand-new to me."

"What are you talking about?"

"Believing."

Somehow the word, the way he spoke it, sounded like the destination on a desperate journey. Why did it feel as if she'd never experienced that word, or the intensity behind it, before? "If you didn't already believe, then why were you in the ministry? Why did you have to come…" She let the words trail off. It would be easier to say nothing than to speak the words "into my life," which would burn her tongue and her soul.

"Not in God. I always believed in Him. I mean in people."

He said it so simply, as if she was supposed to have the foggiest idea what he was talking about. How did allowing Charity to get the best of him— and her—make him believe in people? It didn't make any sense, and she told him so.

"You don't understand," he said. "I really believe that Hannah will tell the truth."

"You're betting your career, your reputation— and mine—on that assumption?"

For a long time he said nothing. Her anger over his naiveté didn't stay long, but worry filled the void it left. Had she gone too far? Had she hurt him terribly? The fact that he'd hurt her suddenly became an historical aside rather than a critical fact. She still couldn't bear to have hurt him. When he finally spoke, his words were little more than a whisper.

"I couldn't tell. You know that."

"Maybe you were bound by some privacy clause to keep Hannah's secret, but you could have told Reverend Bob."

"I was tempted. It even seemed like a good thing to do, on some level. But how could it be fair when it meant revealing Hannah's secret to her father? It wasn't my right to tell."

"Reverend Bob has the right to know, and you have an obligation to tell him."

"No, Serena. I feel certain that God wants me to trust. And He wants me to give Hannah the chance to tell her father about her mistakes, in her time."

"You're taking an awfully big risk."

"I'm just trusting. I wish you would, too. Everything will turn out. Our reputations will be cleared. Hannah will do the right thing. I know it.''

She felt dread on his behalf, even if he wasn't smart enough to feel it. ''What if she doesn't?''

''I have to believe in her.''

''Then, you're a fool.'' She slammed down the phone. Disgust, frustration or fear—or some stirred-up mess of the three—made her want to scream. He'd spent his life questioning everyone. Why did he have to pick one terrified child as his test case for trusting human beings? How could he be that naive?

A plan sparked in her cerebrum, and she had it fully developed before she'd even called her neighbor to baby-sit. Andrew might have placed his trust in the wrong place, might have been bound by a sense of duty to protect church members' privacy. But *she* was restricted by no such rule. She loved him too much to let him wallow in this grave, even if he was the one holding the spade and was the first to break ground.

She grabbed her keys and met Mrs. Nelson at the front door. Yes, someone would help Andrew today. It just wouldn't be the person he expected.

So this was what utter despair felt like. How strange that Andrew didn't recognize those feelings from his past, where they should have been as plentiful as his internalized criticisms. It had been different then. His survival had depended on his not letting those very emotions hold him back. How could he go forward in a life without Serena in it? No, he couldn't think about that now, with this dark hour ahead of him. After that, when all of his worst predictions were memories, he could mourn.

He'd been right. He'd ended up disappointing everyone he'd ever loved, Serena most of all. When early news of his disgrace reached his parents, they'd be reassured their dire predictions for him had been correct. He'd even failed God on a regular basis, but he had to believe this wasn't one of those times.

Serena couldn't understand his decision. How could he blame her? He'd been too much of a coward to tell her he loved her before. And there couldn't have been a more inappropriate time than during that telephone conversation, while she'd been so angry with him.

When he told her—if he ever could now—he wanted it to be when he was close enough to read her heart's response in her eyes. And he doubted he'd ever get that close again. Maybe his plan would have made more sense to her if she could have seen his words through the certainty of knowing she was loved.

Loved. If she could only know how much. He let his mind wander, realizing that after today those thoughts would forever be beyond his reach. In his dreams, Serena would be there in his arms, where she belonged.

He could see her in their kitchen, sitting at the table while he finished his newly famous waffles.

Tessa would be there, too, racing around the table with no pain or stiffness to slow her down. A closer look at Serena would reveal a baby suckling at her breast—their child, with all of her sweetness and his determination combined.

His thoughts drifted further to a night under the crescent moon's glow. Serena would lead him to their room, where their lovers' dreams would combine with marital bliss. Their vows would hold them until heaven's reward.

Andrew shook his head to stop the images. It hurt too much to think about promises that couldn't be kept. He wanted it all so badly, but felt it slipping away.

"Lord, give me the strength to do the right thing, even if it means losing…everything," he whispered. "Please give me peace in my choice." The peace arrived quickly, fortifying his self-doubt. God's will would be done, and it would be the most perfect way.

"Andrew," Reverend Bob called from the other side of partially closed the door. He popped his head inside. "The deacons are waiting."

The right path was often a lonely one, seldom cleared of brush and always bumpy. That wasn't a new revelation. He'd been telling the kids that for months. In his own experience, though, he'd never realized just how far away everyone else could seem or how much pain each step could cause. It was at least in part for the kids who'd listened to him that

Andrew straightened his shoulders and stepped onto the path. It would be the hardest walk of his life.

Had the church's conference room ever looked so huge and unwelcoming before? Andrew knew one thing for certain. The dark wood conference table that stretched the breadth of the room had grown three feet—or ten. Either that or the church had added more deacons to the nine men he'd come to know so well in the past several months.

He stood in the doorway while several heads remained bowed in prayer. Although he'd been in this room dozens of times, he'd somehow missed until now how poorly lit it was. A painting of Jesus surrounded by children was situated above the fireplace, but it was too dark to see the smile on His face.

As the deacons lifted their heads, it was obvious when each of them acknowledged his presence because they stiffened to the straight posture of judgment. Near the south wall, Charity sat, looking appropriately upset.

"Come in, Brother Andrew." Head Deacon David Littleton, seated at the center of the line of men, gestured for him to enter. "Have a seat here in the front, where we can talk."

Andrew sat in the front row of empty folding chairs. To his left was Reverend Bob, out of the line of power but available for input.

"Brother Andrew, Sister Sims has placed a serious charge before us—that you have had a sinful relationship with a church member, Mrs. Jacobs, and that you are unrepentant.'' Deacon Littleton cleared his throat awkwardly. ''How do you respond to her accusation?''

Andrew pressed his lips together, waiting for the appropriate words to come. Nothing could have made it past the stone lodged in his throat, even if he found the right thing to say.

The church's most powerful administrator frowned at him. ''Should I take it from your silence that you have no words to defend yourself? Let me pose my question another way. Have you been involved in sin with Mrs. Jacobs?''

No matter what higher ground Andrew had planned to tread, no matter what words he'd chosen not to say, Andrew couldn't bring himself to lie. ''No, and I cannot allow Serena's reputation to be harmed.''

A few of the other men murmured to each other before trapping Andrew in the intensity of their gazes. If he'd been guilty, he wouldn't have been able to withstand this scrutiny. But he had nothing to hide—only things he couldn't reveal yet.

''Your defense of this woman you obviously have feelings for is honorable, Andrew, but you will need to explain the situation that resulted in Sister Charity witnessing you in such a compromising state.'' Deacon Littleton crossed his arms over his chest. ''You were leaving Mrs. Jacobs's home in the early hours of the morning, after obviously having spent the night there.''

"I don't deny that assertion, but beyond that, I'm afraid I have to delay—not decline—revealing more information than that. Circumstances prevent me from divulging that information until a later time."

Deacon Littleton planted his hands on the desk in frustration. "You are not in a position to make that determination, Mr. Westin. Don't you realize that your position with the church—not to mention your relationship with our Lord—is in jeopardy?"

"If I had another option, I'd take it. But since I don't, I'm only doing what I must."

Deacon Littleton's jaw flexed and his face reddened. "What you *must* do is answer our questions now, or we will be forced to make a decision without your defense. That is something we don't wish to do, but we will do what we must. For as the Scriptures tell us, if a congregation member is found to be in sin by a brother and still does not repent, then his sin is brought to the attention of the body, which has the authority to cast him out."

Reverend Bob approached the long table. "I would like to intercede on Andrew's behalf. My heart instructs me to believe him. Would it be possible to wait a few days to make this decision? Then the answers might be present."

Shock registered on several faces along the table. Charity didn't even bother to hide hers. It was significant for Reverend Bob to step forward this way, with so much circumstantial evidence against Andrew.

"I'm not sure that's possible, Reverend," Deacon

Littleton answered. He turned back to Andrew. "I would like to give you a last opportunity to defend yourself."

Andrew's pulse sped up. Hope slipped away as if fingers had encircled his neck and were slowly squeezing. Last chance. He had only to tell the truth, and everything would be fine. The truth would set him free. But Hannah deserved the chance to reveal her secret in her own time. He couldn't take that away from her, any more than he could question the Father's will here.

Andrew stood and faced his future. "I'm sorry, David, but I cannot speak at this moment. I am bound by my honor and my position not to reveal this confidence."

"Fortunately I'm bound by neither of those things."

Serena's voice brought Andrew around with a start. Instead of looking at him, she stared past him and walked toward the table. Shocked expressions and uncomfortable whispers filled the room. No one spoke aloud, though, as if they expected Deacon Littleton to take charge of the awkward situation. He didn't disappoint them.

"Mrs. Jacobs, this is a private meeting," Deacon Littleton said. "So, if you'll kindly—"

"I'm afraid I can't leave because I am equally accused in this…situation." Serena flashed Charity a look that could never have been misconstrued as forgiving. "If Mr. Westin can't—or won't—defend himself or me, then I feel responsible for doing it myself.''

Andrew moved toward her, hoping to somehow convince her she was making a mistake. From the tight flex of her jaw to the rigidity of her posture, he sensed her fury. And he knew he'd lost Serena, along with his hope. Having the best justification for not telling Hannah's secret didn't seem enough anymore. He'd ask God to forgive him later for losing his fortitude, but now he simply wanted to collapse.

''Please don't tell.'' He touched her arm, but she shook it away. ''It will come to light soon, I promise.''

She turned on him. ''How can you promise? How can you place so much trust in—''

''I have to believe, just as you have always believed in me.'' *Until now.* He wanted to yell the words to reflect his own sense of betrayal. Serena was one of only a few who'd ever believed in him. Or so he'd thought. She hadn't considered him a failure, a disappointment. And now look. She didn't believe in him at all, perhaps hadn't all along. That near-profession of love must have come at a weak moment when she'd needed a masculine shoulder to lean on. He couldn't be that shoulder for her, not anymore.

The anger disappeared from her face, but she still looked determined. ''You're making this suicide leap out of some misguided sense of loyalty. Even if you're bound by some privilege clause, you could still confide in the Reverend, your own spiritual adviser. I can't allow you to ruin yourself, or the both of us.''

Disillusioned, Andrew appealed to her once more. ''Please, Serena, don't do this. It isn't your place.''

''No, it's not.'' The small voice came from the back of the room. Hannah stood there with her hands across her abdomen, perhaps protecting her secret for one last crucial moment. ''But it's mine.''

Chapter Fifteen

The room erupted into a sea of voices, the walls vibrating with a barrage of sound waves. The action around Serena seemed to be occurring in slow motion. Reverend Bob had been on his feet when she'd rushed through the door, but now he pushed past other bodies toward his child at the rear of the room.

What had she done? What had she been thinking when she'd rationalized that causing this scene would be for the best? She'd flown in here like some comic-book heroine, trying to right the world's wrongs on a quick flyby. Shame shrouded her in its darkness.

She glanced over at Andrew, who was like a tower of cards, collapsing into his seat. He buried his face in his hands, likely sending thanks to heaven. Why hadn't she thought to pray first? Once again, she'd ripped the reins of the situation from the Father's hands, so certain she knew what she was doing. The fact that she knew nothing was glaringly obvious. How many lives and how much dignity had she been willing to sacrifice to protect Andrew from himself? The fact that she loved him more than her ability for rational thought was no excuse.

Serena blinked away the surreal feeling about the room and tried to focus on the reality at its center. Everyone here would be affected by today's events. For some, Andrew's faith would strengthen theirs, for others, Serena's lack of it would make them question. It ripped at her heart that she would cause anyone to be uncertain.

Reverend Bob, now simply Bob Woods, the father, folded Hannah into his arms. He took charge of the chaos the same way he led his congregation in worship. "I'm taking my daughter into my office to talk. The rest of you, please wait here."

When he came near Serena, he looked at her with compassion she didn't come close to deserving. A lump formed in her throat. All this time she'd been worrying about her own misery and Andrew's self-destruction. She should have been thinking about the young girl who was facing her darkest moment. Or about the father dealing with the kind of helplessness that Serena knew so well. Why had her compassion taken so long to overcome her selfishness?

Reverend Bob's words interrupted her thoughts.

"Mrs. Jacobs, I'm sure you'll want to get home to your daughter. Thank you for coming."

She didn't deserve his thanks, nearly sacrificing

his daughter. Would he forgive her once he knew the whole truth? She wasn't sure she could forgive herself and, looking at the broken man across the room, she wondered if Andrew ever could, either.

The thought weighed upon her as she walked out of the conference room. Unable to stop herself, she glanced back at the man who owned her heart. If only she could reclaim every word she'd said. Or she could remove the stark betrayal she'd seen in Andrew's eyes. This idiocy had been for him—at least, she hoped it had been for him and not to protect her own reputation. But motives didn't matter anymore. It was too late for that…for anything.

Andrew remained in the chair, seeming to focus on a spot on the wall. Instead of standing tall in the confirmation that his faith had been well-placed, he curled his shoulders forward in defeat. She longed to rush to him, to wrap him in her arms. But she could no more do that than she could deny that everything was different now. Some burned bridges could never be rebuilt.

He never looked back at her. Finally, she turned and walked down the hallway, her energy slipping with each step she took away from him. She passed the sanctuary to the double glass doors that had always invited entry into God's house. The door closed with a heavy *thunk,* as Serena said goodbye to her dreams of a life that might have been.

Later in the afternoon, Andrew shook hands with the nine deacons by turn, nodding at their words of encouragement, their apologies for the difficult situation. He gripped each hand with sincerity, knowing they'd only been doing their duty. Still, he wondered if it would be possible for all of them to rebuild trust.

Behind the church leaders in line, Charity stepped before him, tears trickling down her face. The temptation to refuse to shake her hand was overwhelming, so he called on outside strength to assist him where he was helpless.

She wiped the back of her hand over her eyes. "I'm so sorry, Andrew. I should have given you—you both—the chance to explain."

"I know that you only did what you thought was right." *And what you thought could hurt Serena and me.* He shook away the unforgiving thought. The point was moot. Her decision to come forward could have been motivated by jealousy or revenge—or even sincere commitment to the Word, for that matter—but it no longer mattered. The story had been told. Accusations had been made, and names had been cleared. It was over.

Charity bit her bottom lip. "It was more than that, and you know it."

He only nodded and squeezed her hand before releasing it. That was between Charity and God. Andrew would forgive her as his Lord had forgiven him.

Would the situation involving Hannah have played out differently if Charity had not staked out Serena's home that morning to witness their alleged indiscretion? He wondered how long Hannah would have waited to tell if she'd had the luxury of time. But it did no good to wonder. There was no way this difficult information could have emerged in a perfect light.

Her head low, Charity walked toward the door and called his name over her shoulder. "I know you believe you were doing the right thing by not telling Hannah's secret. I bet Serena thinks the same thing about her actions." She hesitated as if the next words were too difficult to say. "She did it because she loves you."

Her words only added to the strangeness of this day. He couldn't imagine a less likely source. Coming from Charity, the statement should have hurt less. But he only sensed it more keenly, as if the knife that had pierced his flesh were being sawed back and forth deep inside him. If this was what being loved felt like, then he didn't want any part of it. He was glad she left then, without expecting him to respond.

The door to Reverend Bob's office squeaked open, just as it had done an hour before when Bob and Hannah had emerged to make their announcement before the deacons. Everyone had nodded in understanding, seeming to realize what a difficult situation Andrew had been in.

Now that the deacons each had left for home, Hannah came out of the office a second time, her eyes swollen from tears, and rushed forward to hug Andrew. "Thank you for believing in me."

Reverend Bob placed his left arm around his daughter's shoulders and shook hands with Andrew. "Thank you for being there for Hannah."

Andrew nodded. "It was a privilege. Will you two be all right?"

Bob smiled. "We'll be fine. My daughter and I just have a lot to talk about."

They walked out the door arm in arm. At least he'd done one thing right. Andrew walked into the empty sanctuary, allowing the sound-muffling rear door to close behind him. "Thank you, Father, for the strength to do the unpopular thing."

He listened to the way his voice carried through the room. It was that same echo of sound that had always made him feel close to God as a child, even when his mother was flicking him on the shoulder for not paying attention. "Thank you for giving Hannah the strength to come forward. Please give me understanding where I haven't yet found any, and the ability to forgive when I can't do it alone. Amen."

How could he forgive Serena when she'd so blatantly betrayed him? Did she even want him to forgive her? She'd seemed so unapologetic. But Charity had said she believed Serena loved him.

He used to believe the same thing, but now he had only questions and no answers. If she loved him, that scene earlier had been a strange way to show it. She didn't believe in him at all. Wasn't believing the same thing as loving? Worse yet, he wasn't sure he could ever believe in *her* again.

He walked out of the church and locked the double doors. The sun had set on one of those end-of-summer days, where the lack of daylight resulted in an immediate loss of warmth. But his chill started on the inside and worked its way out. As he jogged across the freshly mowed grass to his home, he couldn't help believing that he'd just left his heart on the church steps.

Serena had finally gotten her first taste of sleep, when she heard the knock. At first, she thought it was just the pounding inside her head. Of too many silent tears. Of hundreds of self-destructive thoughts.

But it just kept coming until it pulled her into full consciousness, while from her bedroom window she could still see the magenta remnants of dawn. Her heart beat in her throat as she threw on a robe and headed downstairs. Andrew was going to forgive her. He had to.

It was strange how easily she'd forgiven him for what she'd first thought of as betrayal. He'd never intended to hurt her or her reputation. If only she could have seen that then.

"Hello, Serena."

The disappointment of seeing Trent's face instead of Andrew's put her off balance. That was before the implication of her former husband's presence shoved her back against the doorjamb. She clutched the moldings on both sides to still her trembling limbs.

Pull yourself together. This was no time to show

weakness. She needed to fight. Tessa's heart was at stake, and she couldn't let Trent hurt her again. "How dare you show up here like this?" She stepped out on the porch and closed the door behind her.

Trent looked determined. "I had no choice after you hung up on me. Tessa's my daughter, too. I have every right to see her."

Serena stared at the man who was at the same time both so familiar and an utter stranger. Where there should have been emotion, she felt only numbness. She tightened the belt to close her robe. If only it were that easy to lock Trent out of their lives forever.

"Now that she's healthy, right?"

"What are you implying? I have always—"

"Save your words. I was there. When she was really sick, when her skin was on fire night after night, when we didn't know if the next battery of medical tests was going to give her a death sentence, you couldn't get far enough away from her."

She waited for his caustic response, but it didn't come. Trent just shoved his hands back through his hair and stared at the cars parked along the street.

Serena pressed forward before she could start feeling sorry for him. "You were happy with your picture-perfect family that fit better in a frame on your desk than in real life. But when Tessa got sick, your world collapsed, and you ran away as fast as you could."

She braced herself for a fight she had to win. But

instead of taking a boxer's stance, Trent seemed to collapse into a heap on the porch steps. He squeezed his eyes shut and pinched the bridge of his nose. When he finally spoke again, his voice was shaky.

"She was just so tiny…and so sick." He buried his face in his hands. "My little girl was hurting, and I couldn't make it any better."

His words struck Serena like a two-by-four to the gut. She dropped into one of the painted cast-iron porch chairs. Why had she never sensed his pain before? He was Tessa's father. He loved her. How had Serena assumed that her own agony on Tessa's behalf was somehow superior to his?

But that answer was obvious. It had been easier to believe he didn't care. It justified her refusing to forgive him. She studied him now, broken and lost. She wanted to look away, but his gaze connected with hers.

"I couldn't take it." He shook his head. "I couldn't bear to hear her sob anymore or to see the disappointment in your eyes. So I—"

Serena leapt up and paced to the far end of the porch. "I don't need to hear this—"

"I think you do." He sat in the opposite chair from where she had just gotten up. "I turned to Dawn for comfort, for a nonjudgmental ear."

"And more, if I remember correctly," she said sarcastically.

"I'm happy for you that you're perfect and you can be so smug judging me. I'm not perfect—I know I'm incredibly flawed, in fact—but I'm still Tessa's dad. The court, besides awarding me the opportunity to pay child support, granted me visitation. If you're going to fight me on this, we'll be back in court before—''

''No.'' She couldn't allow this to end up in a court case—one she would lose. Anyway, he was right. For the first time, she saw the past through Trent's eyes. Instead of malevolence, she saw suffering.

Also for the first time, she recognized that she'd had some part in causing that suffering. While she'd been so focused on their child, had she ever bothered to notice Trent's pain? No, all she'd done was criticize him for his weakness. Had that honored him in any way? Cherished him? Loved him? The weight of her guilt made answers unnecessary. She might not have been guilty of violating her marriage vows, but she hadn't done a lot to uphold them, either.

Adding that accusation to the growing list of self-condemnation pushed her to the edge. She'd done everything else wrong, losing so much in the process. She just had to get this right. Not for herself this time, but for Tessa.

''Wait here a minute.'' She closed the door and climbed the stairs, the burning behind her eyes promising tears. Her chest was so heavy that she wasn't sure she could bear it, until she entered the doorway of her sleeping child. Was she about to make another huge mistake in which Tessa would be the victim?

Tessa's eyes fluttered open when Serena gently sat on the bed next to her. "Good morning, Mommy. I woke up."

"Yes, you did. Now I have a surprise for you." She opened her arms wide and Tessa climbed into them.

She carried her downstairs and out the front door. "Surprise."

"Daddy, Daddy." Tessa climbed down, running from one parent to the other. There was no sign of residual hurt, only joy.

Serena wanted to feel that for her, too. If she were less selfish, she would because Tessa deserved to have a father in her life. But it was so hard to feel anything at all while her heart was being slowly, torturously rent in two.

Serena managed to hold it together through the morning visit, a grilled cheese lunch, Trent's departure and preparation for Tessa's nap, before she finally lost it. The urge to run was overwhelming as she made her way to her own room, through that tiny door inside her bedroom closet and into that private room behind it where she could cry alone. Where Tessa wouldn't hear her.

"*Lord, please…*" The words were but a whisper, a plea.

Suddenly her gaze fell on a box of books pushed up against the wall. On top was her old study Bible, so frayed from usage that the edges of its gold pages were now a dull yellow. She touched it with her fingertips, caressing the worn leather. Then she lifted it to her face so she could breathe in the stale scent of aging paper.

It was strange how the Scriptures comforted her, even closed. She smiled down at the Bible. How funny that she used to believe if she allowed the pages to fall open, God would provide a Scripture she needed to read. She held the book between her palms a few seconds longer, shrugged and let the pages fall.

The Book of Psalms appeared before her, so close to the center of the Bible. She was about to laugh at the statistical likelihood of that—until her gaze fell to the words printed in Psalm 55. "Cast your burden on the Lord, and He will sustain you; He will never permit the righteous to be moved."

A tune slipped into her consciousness: the old church camp song that used the words of the Psalm. She swayed to its melody in her mind. Young campers had encouraged each other to cast their burdens during a time when they still had so few of them. Today she was filled to bursting with them.

Lord, I can't do it anymore. I don't want to do it anymore. I'm tired. She didn't even try to wipe away her tears. It was easier to let them fall. *I've tried so hard. I wanted to control every situation— with Tessa, with Trent, with Andrew. And I've handled them all horribly. I've failed Tessa. I've failed Andrew. And most of all, I've failed you, Father.*

She'd never been in control, anyway. And she'd botched everything whenever she'd tried to be. She was only making it official now by handing over the reins. *Lord, show me the way, and I will follow.*

On Saturday morning Andrew tucked his meager possessions into the last of a dozen boxes, most of them containing books. He glanced at the envelope propped next to the door. At least no one had noticed the letter the day before when it appeared on the church's community printer. It would be hard enough to deliver his notice without having his secret leak out before he was ready.

Just the thought of resigning was enough to send his stomach into a barrel roll. How would he face Reverend Bob? He didn't want to leave at all. His was more than a job. It was his ministry, his life. But he had no choice. The water that had passed under this bridge was as polluted as the River Nile after God's plague against the Egyptians had turned it to blood.

How could the Reverend Bob, the deacons and himself—let alone Charity and the rest of the congregation—reconcile themselves after this? Forgiving was one thing. The Scriptures demanded it, and he would comply. But forgetting—that was different. Could he really blank those ugly moments out of his mind forever and go back to teaching the same kids who were aware of those dark times? Could he ever trust again?

Unbidden, the image of Serena addressing the deacons appeared in his mind. How could he ache in this many places at once? And how could each spot hurt equally, as if they were in some cruel competition? Still, he couldn't justify in his mind what she'd done. She'd listened to the words from his soul and then betrayed him as if she hadn't heard him at all.

He'd always expected love to be like this—full of mistrust rather than selflessness. He'd been right to avoid it for most of his life. But Serena had come along, and he'd tossed away his reason. She'd stepped into his protected world, and it had spontaneously combusted.

He'd been certain Serena was right for him. How could his heart, his soul have been so wrong? The wonder of it all was that his heart still betrayed him. He loved her…even now. There was nothing he could do about it. She'd called him a "fool." He hated knowing she was right.

What about the words she'd almost said? She loved him—at least, she'd nearly said she did. She'd even seemed hurt when he couldn't respond in kind. He wished he could believe her words were only part of the huge mind game she'd been playing. But his heart wouldn't let him.

Even Charity, who'd had nothing to gain, believed Serena had approached the deacons because she loved him. Why else would she have done it? If she'd been worried about her own reputation, she easily could have chosen another church among the many in Milford.

He was the one whose reputation—and livelihood—depended on the truth being revealed. She'd done it for him. Her action showed she loved him. If that was the kind of love she offered, he'd just as soon stay alone, thank you.

Alone. That was exactly what he'd be after he gave that letter to Reverend Bob. Without the friends he'd made here. Without Tessa, the child he'd come to love as his own. Without Serena.

No, he couldn't think about that now. He needed to focus on what he had to do. Reverend Bob wanted to meet with him today, anyway. The minister tended to hole up in his office on Saturday mornings to put the final touches on his sermons. They'd be the only two there, so this was as good a time as any for him to resign.

Later, when he was far from here, he could think about what might have been and wallow in regret over losing everything that was important to him in this world.

Chapter Sixteen

Reverend Bob was on the telephone, but motioned Andrew into his office, anyway. "Thank you for calling, Mrs. Henderson. I'll add your mother to the prayer list in the bulletin."

Ignoring the nerves inside his abdomen, Andrew pulled the envelope from his back pocket and set it on the Reverend's desk. There was no use tiptoeing around this issue. He'd do what he came here to do, cram some of his stuff in his car and go. Where, he had no idea.

It was an unfortunate characteristic of his profession, which specialized in forgiveness, that it also was a career where one's past haunted the future. His involvement in a scandal, whether his name had been cleared or not, probably would follow him wherever he went.

"So, Andrew." Reverend Bob leaned back in his

chair and steepled his hands across his chest. "I'm glad we've finally got this chance to talk."

Finally? It had been only two days since that special-call deacons' meeting and the eye-opening of his life regarding love. Two very long days. Andrew stared at the envelope on the minister's desk, hoping Reverend Bob would notice it. But Bob either didn't catch the hint, or he was purposely trying not to.

"I guess we had to, sometime."

Reverend Bob leaned forward on the desk, resting on his elbows. "I wanted to thank you again for being such a good friend to my daughter. When Hannah needed someone, you were there to listen to her, and I am so grateful."

Andrew shook his head. "I was just doing my job." If that was all it was, then why was his memory so vivid of that sobbing child sandwiched between Serena and him, the two of them absorbing her agony? It was while giving to another together that he'd felt closest to Serena. And it was because of that same situation that they were now apart.

"You and I both know it was more than that." Reverend Bob paused, staring out the window. "What you and Serena did for Hannah...I don't know what would have happened to her without you."

Andrew jerked his head to look at the Reverend. Was his memory selective? "How can you say that about us? Serena was even willing to sacrifice Hannah to protect her reputation and mine."

"I don't see that at all."

"What do you mean?"

Reverend Bob smiled the expression of a man who held all the answers. "In the years I've been at the pulpit, I've been amazed at the lengths people will go when protecting someone they love."

"If that's love—" Reverend Bob shook his head to silence Andrew. "You can't see how lucky you are. A woman loved you enough to risk losing you, by protecting you from yourself."

Andrew pressed his fingers against his skull. "She didn't believe in me. Just when I finally learned to believe in others, she couldn't believe in *me*." Rounding his desk, Reverend Bob rested a hand on Andrew's shoulder. "Despite the hurt she has caused you, you still love her."

Andrew shook his head, not wanting to believe it, let alone acknowledge it to someone else. Loving her showed he had no self-preservation skills, no common sense.

Reverend Bob crossed his arms. "Will you deny you love her and lie to me, here in our Lord's house?"

Andrew stared at the wall. He needed to escape, but there was no place to go. "I love her. But I can't see what difference that makes now."

Reverend Bob smiled. "Just as God's love is the difference between an eternity in glory or misery, love can make all of the difference in the world."

What could he say to that? Could any words express the blown-glass quality of his heart, its ability to splinter into millions of fragments? Should he even risk hoping that Reverend Bob might be right?

Andrew shook that nonsense away. Hope was dangerous. They'd come too far to look back now. To survive, he had to walk away with what little pride he had left.

He had to get out of here and race to someplace where he could breathe again. To someplace where he didn't have to imagine her face, remember the floral scent of her hair or feel her nearness on the surface of his skin. Was there any such place?

Reverend Bob tapped a pencil on his desk in a nervous rhythm. ''I took Hannah to the doctor yesterday. They confirmed that she's pregnant.''

Andrew's thoughts jerked back to the young woman whose life was in turmoil and to the parent forced to watch his child's pain. Guilt for his selfishness filled him. ''What has Hannah chosen to do…about the pregnancy?''

Reverend Bob waved his hand in a dismissive gesture. ''She'll have the baby, of course.'' His words were confident. But his commanding presence and straight posture seemed to have been stripped from him. He dropped his head into his hands and was quiet a long time before he spoke again. ''My little girl will be giving birth to a child of her own. She's so young.''

''Will she keep the baby?'' Andrew was surprised at the way the word *baby* caught in his throat. Again, he saw that infant of his dreams nestled in Serena's arms. He tried hard to focus on the mother of this particular child. Hannah deserved more than his wandering mind was giving her.

"Hannah hasn't decided yet whether to raise her child herself or grant that privilege to adoptive parents."

"Has she said anything about the father?" Andrew hated himself as soon as he'd said the words, but he couldn't help but wonder.

"She refuses to tell. She's adamant about it. I think she's protecting the boy, but I'm not pressing."

Andrew nodded. "It's just as well. At least you won't have another family involved in the decision-making."

A flash of guilt passed through his mind, but its journey was a fast one. Yes, he had a pretty good idea who the second parent was to this new life. His identity, though, didn't seem like the most important thing right now. Hannah would just deny it, anyway.

Hadn't Hannah lost enough? Her mother, her childhood, her purity, and most likely her love. The least he could do for her was allow her to keep Todd as her one secret. For a reason he couldn't explain— perhaps a seed of the trust he'd guessed was gone forever—he was certain that Serena would never tell, either.

"You're right." Reverend Bob stood up—maybe not as straight as usual, but he squared his shoulders, anyway. "You know, none of those things matters right now—her ultimate decision about adoption or even the boy involved."

Reverend Bob paced with the nervous energy of a man faced with critical decisions. "What matters is Hannah. I won't worry about being a grandfather to this child who is still months away from greeting the world. Right now, I have to focus on being a *father* to my daughter. I want to be the parent she really needs now."

Andrew walked to his friend and hugged him. Reverend Bob needed support as much as Hannah did. He'd experienced more pain than Andrew could even have seen in his worst nightmares. The woman Bob loved had passed from this earth instead of simply from his life. Now he was helpless to ease his child's pain. And still he believed. Andrew hoped one day to have that strong a faith.

"Hannah's a very lucky girl to have a dad like you. I'll pray for the both of you. God has a plan here."

Reverend Bob smiled. "He has a plan for you, too. You just need to figure out what it is."

Andrew nodded and looked down at the desk. "Bob, aren't you going to look at the letter?"

For the first time in their conversation, the older man glanced at the envelope on the desktop. "I'm pretty busy today preparing for tomorrow's service. How about I look at it Monday? We'll talk about it then."

Andrew returned to his makeshift apartment to take the time Reverend Bob had hinted he needed, but the walls closed in on him more with each passing hour. Still, he sat in the recliner, a captive of his thoughts.

The minister just didn't get it. He couldn't possibly have understood what it was like to live a life where no one believed in him, where everyone expected failure from him and he'd felt powerless to do anything but fulfill their prophesy.

Serena had been different. At least, he'd thought she was different. Her artificial belief in him had inspired him to believe in others, and that had only resulted in misery. Andrew pushed his back into the well-worn upholstery, taking in the physical sensation of wallowing in self-pity. He deserved this. With all he'd lost, he planned to take full advantage of the opportunity to feel sorry for himself.

Did you really believe? The thought immediately put him on the defensive. Of course he'd begun to have faith in people. Otherwise, why would he have hung himself out to dry while waiting for Hannah to do the right thing? He'd been confident she'd tell the truth—was positive of it. Now he had no regrets.

Except that he was here in this room that was for nothing more than storage, while Serena was on the other side of town suffering for doing what she'd thought was right. *Did you really believe?* He didn't want to hear that question again. It was beginning to incriminate him.

Could he truly say that he'd trusted in people when he'd ripped that faith away as soon as one had failed to meet his expectations? What if God offered salvation that same way—withdrawing the offer whenever a sinner failed to live up to His perfect example? Heaven would be a pretty empty place. If the Father could forgive Andrew's lifetime of failings, then he should have been able to forgive at least one trespass. If he couldn't, then he'd never believed in people at all. And how could he say his faith in God was real if he couldn't trust in His creations?

Serena's face appeared in his thoughts again. He could still see the feminine way her mouth softened when he was about to kiss her. His heart tripped the way it had at the first sound of her voice inside his office. They loved each other. That was true, no matter how loudly he denied it. It meant everything and nothing at the same time. His heart still leaped at the melodic memory of her voice, while being crushed by the impact of her words.

As futile as anger was now—with himself, with situations beyond his control—he indulged himself, gripping the chair's armrests so hard that he probably made permanent indentations. But it wasn't enough. Nervous energy had him up and pacing. That didn't help, either. He stood at the window, looking out across the grassy field.

His emptiness wasn't about to disappear, he realized, as long as he remained trapped within this room's shrinking walls. With all of his inner strength, he forced himself to head outside. He didn't know what was ahead as he jogged to the barn and kick-started the motorcycle. There was no turning back now.

* * *

"Mommy, can I have two daddies?"

Serena hadn't realized how far she'd slipped away from Tessa's bubble bath, until the question ripped her back. "What are you talking about, angel-cookie?"

"Well, I have you, and Daddy says that Mrs. Dawn is a second mommy for me. Can Mr. Andrew be my second daddy? I want to have two daddies, too."

Serena grabbed a handful of bubbles and blew them through the air in a vain attempt to calm her trembling insides. As difficult as it was to think of Tessa spending time with a stepmother, it wasn't that particular bridge Serena was most reluctant to cross. Admitting to Tessa there would be no future with Andrew was the same as accepting it herself. The thought drained her.

"I'm sorry, honey. I don't think it's going to work out that way."

"It's really easy, Mommy. Daddy told me that when he married Mrs. Dawn, she became my stick mommy. All you have to do is marry Mr. Andrew, and he can be my stick daddy."

Serena chuckled. She thanked the Lord for Tessa and for the optimism of childhood. Tessa's presence would be one of God's gifts in the days to come, providing Serena with a boost when she felt hopeless. Tessa had so much stacked against her, yet she always viewed life with promise. If only Serena could be as strong. Even now, she fought against tears that were becoming as much a habit as breathing; she squeezed her eyes shut to aid in the battle.

Something wet on the end of her nose made her blink them back open. Staring cross-eyed, she saw the bubbles Tessa had deposited there. The tiny love of her life giggled and threw her head back into the bathwater, making another rinse necessary.

"First, honey, you call them step-mommy and step-daddy—not stick. And second, it's not really easy at all." She took the deepest breath she could ever remember taking, and prepared to say the words that would break her own heart again. "You see—"

"Hey, Tess, those bubbles look like a bunch of fun."

Serena froze, her neck too numb to turn toward the voice behind her, the voice of the man so deeply embedded in her soul that she couldn't dare to hope he'd come back for her. With all her strength, she turned toward him, trying to look as impassive as any person about to have a heart attack could.

Andrew grinned and then tried to purse his lips. Any words at all would have been better than the silence that hung between them like the steam from Tessa's bath.

Though the two of them were tongue-tied, when Tessa came out from under the faucet suds-free again, she wasn't as bashful.

"Mr. Andrew, you're here. Mommy doesn't get it. Can you tell her—"

Serena grabbed Tessa out of the tub, wrapping her in a towel before the child could really humiliate her. It was bad enough wondering how much of the conversation Andrew had overheard. She'd have to talk to him about sneaking into the house. She almost laughed at that. She was giddy he was there at all. Butterflies fluttering through her insides ruined her best attempt at appearing casual.

"You know, you should always remember to lock your front door, even in Milford. You never know who might walk in off the street—especially after he rang the bell and banged on the door three times."

He laughed, and she tried her best to laugh back. It sounded so fake that even Tessa looked up at her with a raised eyebrow. She might as well ask. Not knowing was killing her, anyway.

"What—what are you doing here?"

"Mommy, he's come to be my stick, no stepdaddy." Tessa puffed up her shoulders, seeming proud of her announcement. Then she dropped her towel and stood just the way she'd been created.

Andrew tucked the towel back around Tessa's sopping form. He winked—whether at Tessa or herself, Serena couldn't decide. Nothing about this moment was clear.

He had Tessa wrapped like a burrito before he spoke again. "I did come to talk to your mom, if that's okay."

Tessa's expression fell for a second before she

brightened. "Will you read me a story when it's bedtime?"

He rustled her messy mop. "You can count on it."

Serena kept busy dressing Tessa and combing her tangles. It was the only way to stay calm as the minutes ticked by. Soon she'd be alone with Andrew and the issue that stood between them like Mount Everest between two valleys. She didn't even feel guilty for bribing Tessa out of their hair with an extra half-hour of television. There just wasn't space in her mind for more guilt than was crowding every corner of her consciousness.

Once Tessa was comfy, with a plumped pillow and her sleeping bag and seated in front of her show, Serena led Andrew to the porch. She looked at the hard cast-iron chairs and sat instead on the steps. There was something good about being low to the ground. At least then, if her last safety net of hope was ripped away, she wouldn't have so far to fall.

He sat next to her, turning his knees until he faced her. "I thought we should talk."

"I'm so, so sorry, Andrew." She should have predicted it, should have known that the tears would come, with the heat and violence of dashed hopes. The flood surprised her, anyway.

Andrew looked at Serena, really looked for the first time since he'd barged into her house. Her tears tore at his heart with angry claws. But her anguish was only the surface of what he saw. The skin beneath her eyes was a translucent curtain covering purplish half-moons of sleeplessness.

The need to pull her into his arms was a physical ache inside him, but he felt paralyzed. Not a single limb would move.

"You did what you felt was right," he said. *Because you loved me.* The hopeful side of his heart added the words despite his objection.

"But it was so wrong. You were finally ready to believe in people, and I proved you shouldn't trust in us at all." She hung her head.

Was he being too easy on her? Should he forgive her? He was fooling himself if he didn't face that he had forgiven her a long time ago. "I'm sorry, too, Serena. I wish I'd done things differently. I wish my growth hadn't caused you to be hurt. But the fact is, it did. Everyone has to live with the consequences of choices—even us."

"But do we have to lose everything in the process?"

Her question was so simple, but its answer had the permanence of a life sentence. "I don't know. I just don't know."

The anguish in her eyes was as powerful as her plea. "Please try to forgive me? I've forgiven you."

He stared at his feet, feeling unworthy. It was that forgiving and forgetting catch-22 again. "I don't know why you did forgive. I was perfectly willing to sacrifice your reputation, even if I did have a valid reason."

"It was easy…once I handed it over to God."

Andrew jerked his head up so quickly he pinched his neck. Had he heard her right? Hope sparked before he could douse it.

For the first time in the conversation, she almost smiled. With the back of her hand, she tried to wipe away her tears. He wished he could do it for her. Humiliating pride kept his hands at his sides.

She pressed her lips together. "Maybe it's too late for—whatever—but I finally figured out who needs to be in the driver's seat, and it isn't me. With Tessa's condition, with you, with Trent—"

"What about Trent?" The jealousy that grabbed his insides was as frustrating as it was confusing. Was he also ready to forget now?

"He showed up again, now that Tessa's doing better, and wants to reconnect with his daughter."

"Are you okay?" It was a little unsettling to realize that all of her pasty fragility wasn't about missing him. Had he really wanted her to hurt that way over him?

She nodded. "I'm fine. With God's help, I'm really fine. And Tessa's got her father back, at least for now. Everything is as good as it can be."

Was it? Could it be a whole lot better if he'd let his heart lead instead of his mind? He longed to pull her to him, to connect with her skin the way his heart was already permanently attached to hers. But he couldn't. Something was holding back those words of forgiveness.

After what must have been several minutes, she patted his arm just once before pulling away. His limb warmed where her hand had rested. After to-night, would he ever experience the joy of her touch again? Or would he let his pride prevent him from having the one thing on Earth that he needed most?

"Andrew, I realize we can't fix what is broken between us. What I did was unforgivable. But I want you to know I did it because I love you. And no matter what you've convinced yourself, you are worthy of being loved. I wish you…happiness." She choked then and hurried into the house.

He watched her go, helplessness holding him in its miserable grasp. A better man would have followed. He'd always been a failure, though. It came as no surprise to him that he stayed seated.

He had to get away. To think. To be alone with his thoughts and his God. He had to be sure he was ready to forgive Serena and accept her forgiveness. He had to have enough faith to trust in her fully and enough strength to let her trust him. Was he prepared to give himself the freedom to be happy?

Chapter Seventeen

Numbness seeped through Serena's limbs as effectively as it had captured her mind. Nothing had ever felt more final than the sound of that Harley, roaring out of her life.

Acceptance was an empty thing sometimes. It didn't make its victim feel high or low—just there. That void was hers now. Those tears that had flowed so freely before, had dried. Futile tears.

She pressed her back to the screen door, watching Tessa, who was still engrossed in her show. It took all of her strength not to stare after Andrew, hoping for a last glimpse. But the finality of that would probably kill her.

Well, she'd wanted an answer, had even prayed for one. That God had responded differently than she'd hoped couldn't be an issue now. She'd promised to trust—to cast her burden—and now she was only keeping her word. Her commitment didn't deaden the pain, but it offered the hope that one day her Lord would ease it.

Tessa turned toward her, looking confused. "Mommy, where's Mr. Andrew?"

"He had to leave, honey."

Tessa's tiny lower lip quivered with a prediction of tears. "But he promised to read me a story."

"I know, punky, and I'm sure he really planned to do it. But he really had to leave."

"Will he come back?"

The threatening flood dried in Tessa's eyes. She was accustomed to being disappointed by men. Once again, Serena couldn't protect her.

"No, he won't."

"Will you read me a story, then?"

"Of course I will." She took Tessa's hand and led her upstairs. Just a step at a time. Maybe an unsteady walk was all she could manage today, but the Lord would give her the ability to run again soon.

After tucking her in, Serena started reading Tessa's favorite book, *Good Night Moon.* "'In the great green room, there was a telephone and a red balloon and a picture of—'" She knew those words by heart, but still she tripped on the soothing message when a jarring faraway growl of a motorcycle invaded the house's silence.

It was summer. There were thousands of motorcycles on Michigan roads at this time of year, their riders racing to get the most out of the state's brief riding season. It didn't have to mean… She didn't dare hope again—not now, when it was too late. But the sound grew stronger, the approaching drumroll of impending arrival. She gave in to her curiosity, rushing across the hall to look out her bedroom window. Below, Andrew was parking again where he'd been not thirty minutes before.

She raced down the stairs, but somehow Tessa beat her to the front door. Andrew marched up the steps.

"Mommy, he came back to read me my story!"

"You bet I did, Tess." Andrew led Tessa by the hand upstairs, glancing back at Serena with an unreadable expression. "A deal's a deal."

Serena collapsed on the couch, her heart tripping and her mind dancing over possibilities she had no business imagining. He'd said nothing more than that he was fulfilling a promise. He'd never said he was ready to forgive her—or that he could ever forgive her.

It was amazing how resilient hope was, how it could burn to the ground and sprout again with mere drops of nourishment. She hoped she could survive the trip back down again, if it came.

Soon she heard the baritone sound of Margaret Wise Brown's story being read again. About five minutes later, he returned downstairs and stood in the doorway to the living room. He stared but didn't speak. Serena's ears were so trained for sound that her head ached. Her insides trembled, and the contents of her stomach backed up in her throat. Why didn't he say something? Anything?

Finally, she filled the silence with her own words. "Thanks for coming back to read to Tessa. You made her happy." If he needed her to say it was okay to go, she'd do that, as well.

"I will always be a man of my word…to both of you."

His words brought Serena's head up. *Always?* Before she had the chance to ponder hidden meanings, he crossed the room and held out his hand to her, leading her outside to sit on the porch steps.

"I needed to think, to get my feelings in order. I drove around until I realized the place I needed to be was here." He reached for her hand and laced his fingers with hers. "I realized something tonight. Being right isn't enough."

She shook her head at his confusing words, trying to ignore the comfort she derived from his touch. "What do you mean?"

He squeezed her hand harder. "I was right to put my trust in a seventeen-year-old girl. I was right to have faith in humankind. The Father taught me to believe. You taught me, too."

Serena tried to pull her hand away, but he held firm. "I wish you could forgive—"

"But don't you see? I *have* forgiven you." He paused until she looked at him. "I think I did so the moment you spoke those words to the deacons, although I had a hard time overcoming the hurt."

Serena shut her eyes tightly. Hurting Andrew had been like a knife in her heart. The wound still festered. "I never intended to hurt you."

"And I was wrong to hurt you, just to be right. But what I'm saying is that being right isn't enough—not when I have to wake up every morning without you, when I have to go to sleep each night without tucking Tessa in and helping her say her prayers."

What was he saying? Her thoughts and pulse raced with competing speeds. The need to believe in him battled the fear of risking her heart, the fear losing bit by bit. She couldn't stop it. She didn't even want to. Her future rested on the next words he would say. All she could do was wait like a convicted criminal facing sentencing.

He leaned in close until their gazes met. "I love you, Serena Leigh Daniels Jacobs. I was too afraid to tell you because it would make me vulnerable. It's strange now, how in telling you, I have never felt stronger."

Heat collected behind her eyes before his image blurred. In a gentle caress, he wiped her tears away with his thumbs. He took her hands again.

"I love you, too. More than you know." It felt so wonderful finally to admit the truth. So like a dream that instantly became reality. Saying the words made her feel powerful, even though again she was releasing control.

Andrew pressed a kiss to her palm. "I do know, because I feel the same way. You're the Lord's gift to me. I've been such an ungrateful son. But I'm not going to be anymore. I want to spend the rest of my life cherishing you and thanking the Father for you."

Serena had no time to still the trembling that began in her center and vibrated to her extremities before Andrew gathered her into his arms. She held her breath, thinking that this was one of the most perfect moments in her life. But then he lowered his lips to hers, and the moment before paled into nothingness. His kiss was the seal of a promise, where beginnings flowed into eternity and endings didn't exist.

She lifted her arms around his neck and nestled her fingers in the hair at his nape. Being there, in his arms, felt so right. It was where she should have been all along. Andrew's tender kiss continued on a path of deepening connection, of promised future intimacies, until she was sure she'd melt in a puddle on the porch. She reluctantly pulled away, only to see the haze in Andrew's eyes.

She leaned in once more. Nothing seemed more important than to touch his lips with her own again—

The sound of someone clearing his throat stopped her a breath away from that goal.

Both turned their heads to see Reverend Bob standing awkwardly at the end of the walk, his mouth turned up in an impish grin. "You were right, Andrew. You and Serena should be married. Right away. Sure glad I dropped by today to see Serena."

Serena's face burned, but it was as much from pleasure as embarrassment. Had he really told the minister he wanted to marry her? Did he really want to make her his wife? Impossibility flitted on the edges of certainty, and she waited for the final assurance.

Andrew touched her shoulder. "You see, Bob, I, on occasion, can be incredibly smart."

"Well, then, we'd better set a date. And soon."

"Would you mind waiting inside until I propose to the potential bride? Tessa's been in bed awhile. She's probably asleep, so stay quiet, okay?"

Reverend Bob nodded and stepped through the front door.

Andrew turned back to her and took her hands in his. "Whatdya say, Tessa's mom, could you handle taking on the role of the youth minister's wife, too?"

Serena steadied herself against a battle with tears, certain she'd lost. "As long as when you come home at night, you'll be just Serena's husband and Tessa's *stick* daddy."

"I'll be more than that. I'll be the guy who loves the mommy and loves the little girl as his own."

She smiled up at him. "Then, my answer is yes."

He was about to kiss her but stopped inches from her lips. "I don't have a ring for you yet." He seemed to think for a minute. "For the time being, would you mind wearing this?" He pulled the cross out from under his shirt, unclasped it and then clasped it around her neck.

Serena's breath caught in her throat. With an unsteady hand she brought the cross to her lips. The metal felt cool on one side but warm where it had so recently been touching his skin. It was a symbol of so much more than a proposal made and accepted. Theirs would be a union with God at the center, about promises kept and prayers answered. She didn't need a diamond ring. Their future was best symbolized with that cross.

She lifted the collar of her sleeveless mock turtleneck and dropped the necklace beneath it, so it could be close to her heart. When she looked up again, she saw him drawing closer to her. Then he covered her lips with his own in a kiss of commitment.

A question struck her then, causing her to break off the kiss and earn his moan. "How did you make this leap of understanding, all in a half-hour's time?"

"I was pretty close before. I only needed to take the example from a certain spiritual adviser and turn my problems over to God." He laughed and lifted her hand to his lips. Then he yelled over his shoulder, "Hey Bob, she said 'yes.'"

"Yeah, we know."

They looked up to see Reverend Bob standing at the screen door, holding Tessa in his arms. With a grin, he removed his hand from where it had covered Tessa's mouth.

"Mr. Andrew's going to be my stick daddy!" She climbed down and slipped out the door.

Andrew stood, helping Serena up and lifting Tessa to sit on his hip. "That's right. I guess that makes you Stick Tessa. We'll just be the 'Stick' family...one that sticks together."

Epilogue

Twelve months later

Serena smoothed the comforter into place and pulled the bed skirt until it lay just right. "Perfect."

She studied the room to make sure everything was in its place. The circus theme in primary colors was wonderful, as was that one bright-red accent wall with the clown in the center. All the pieces were put away, ready for the big event: mobile, bumper pads, changing table, diaper stacker, pile of tiny gowns.

A squeal outside drew her attention to the window, where filmy white curtains billowed in the breeze. As usual, she saw a child with a head full of unruly dark curls racing across the yard with a sandy-brown-haired, much taller "kid" chasing behind.

"You can't catch me. I'm too fast for you," Tessa

announced while barely an arm's length from Andrew's grasp.

A sudden accidental fall sent the pursuer sprawling on the ground, bemoaning the failure of his mission. "I just couldn't catch you."

Tessa ran toward him and leaped on his back, not seeming to hear the authentically pained grunt at her landing. "But I can catch *you.*"

In a flash, he flipped over and grabbed her, hugging her against him. "I've got you now."

"Not anymore." She shook away his hands and scampered away. The whole game started over again.

Serena chuckled at the sweet sight and felt a joyful kick from inside her rounded abdomen. With eyes closed, she patted her belly, enjoying that moment of connection with the second child of her heart. Then she gazed out the window at the antics of her first.

Tessa scrambled up the lower limb of their favorite climbing tree. Without hesitation, she stood on the branch and leapt to the ground. Gone was the cautious little girl who'd lived in pain. Now she could focus on the magic of childhood instead of the agony of movement.

Serena cringed when her child's feet hit the ground, expecting Tessa to collapse into a heap. How many months—or years—would she have that same gut reaction whenever her child took a risk? With the brief memory of childhood, Tessa had already forgotten the dark days, the pain, the tears. But Serena was the mother. She'd never forget.

It was amazing to realize that Tessa had been free from any joint inflammation for about a year now. The injections of methotrexate continued to be a weekly battle, but the drug had worked miracles.

Her pediatric rheumatologist had even told them that after Tessa had two years without any joint swelling, they would attempt to wean her from the medication. Even then, she wouldn't be considered "in remission" until she had a year with no medicine and no swollen joints. They had a long road ahead, but it was filled with hope.

"Caught you again." Andrew grabbed his stepdaughter, tossing her over his shoulder like a sack of potatoes. The sound of glee whirled around them.

Tessa was such a lucky little girl. She had a stepfather who adored her and a biological father who had—at least so far—kept his promise to be an involved parent. And, she admitted begrudgingly, Dawn had turned out to be a loving stepmother.

Serena patted her belly again. "You're going to be a lucky kid, too, little one. With a daddy like Andrew and a big sister like Tessa, you just won't be able to help being happy. And, I'll try to be a good mommy, too."

Across the field, a congregation member roared through the church field on a tractor with a wide mowing deck. Beyond the church building, she could see the dusty construction site for the new Family Life Center.

She rested her hands on the frame of the old window, thankful for the millionth time that the congregation had opted, after their wedding just over a year ago, to keep the old house as a second parsonage instead of renovating it for the center. This fringe benefit certainly bolstered Andrew's small salary, making their lives more comfortable.

Okay, so it wasn't ideal living this close to her husband's job, but she loved the house and the life they were building inside it.

She didn't regret for a minute that Andrew had decided to keep his fellowship, which had eventually become a permanent position where he would work daily with Reverend Bob. It was great getting to stay here, spending time with Hannah and her daughter, Rebecca. That little one always had a smile for everyone.

The church community had proven itself a tool of God through its care for Hannah during her pregnancy, even supporting her decision to raise her child. Members had stepped forward, providing her with baby supplies and with child care, so she could complete her senior year and begin college in the fall.

Serena couldn't help wondering why Hannah had never revealed the father's identity. If Todd was the father—and she believed he was—Serena was curious whether Hannah had been protecting him or was angry with him. Hannah certainly never mentioned his name anymore.

Had she ever told Todd about the baby? Could he

possibly have heard from his faraway home in Singapore? Whether or not Hannah ever confided those answers, Serena was glad for her friendship and forgiveness.

She stared out the window at Andrew again, sweating from his workout with Tessa but never admitting defeat. He'd been just as tenacious in his job this year, rebuilding weakened relationships and making sound ones even stronger. She felt good about her role as his partner in that effort and had enjoyed the fringe benefits, including a wonderful new friendship with Reverend Bob. She hoped one day she and Andrew could work together to build some sort of relationship with Andrew's parents, as well.

Tension had eased with the deacons, making her life a lot easier. The only uncomfortable vibes she still felt came from Charity and her mother. She'd placed that situation in God's hands and was working hard to leave it there. She was still anxious about the prospect of Charity being on duty when Serena delivered her baby at West Oakland Regional. As hard as it was, she'd decided to let God take care of that as well.

She returned to her observation from her window perch, thankful for the tiny breeze that gave a reprieve from the day's humidity. On the ground below, Tessa and Andrew had disappeared, probably off on another adventure.

Her mind traveled back to not so long ago—though it seemed like a lifetime ago—when she'd believed her life had been charmed. How wrong she'd been. She didn't even desire a charmed life anymore. Where was the victory in that? Where was the sweetness?

She preferred her life today to that empty perfection—with too little pain to recognize joy, too little faith to touch the divine. Their life together was so much better. It was a blessed life. Every day was a gift. She couldn't have asked for anything more.

"Boo!" Tessa leaped into the room. "We scared you."

Andrew walked up behind Serena, wrapped his arms around her rounded middle and kissed her neck. "Caught you watching us out the window again. What do you think, Tessa, does Mommy like us?"

"She loves us…and baby Preston."

"Preston?" Serena asked with a laugh. "Preston Westin? Where did you get that name?"

"Daddy Andrew thought that one up outside."

"Along with Mortimer Snurd Westin and Dolly Madison Westin." Andrew turned Serena around and bent to lay a kiss on her belly. "We're coming up with our best ideas."

Serena ruffled his hair before he could stand. "I say we'd better keep working on it."

Andrew stepped toward her, speaking just inches from her face. "I say we'll always keep working on it."

She smiled. They were no longer talking about silly baby names. She leaned in to him, her belly getting in the way as she sank her lips into the wonder of his.

"Mommy. Daddy Andrew. I want kisses, too." Tessa tugged at the back of Serena's maternity top.

Andrew reached down and lifted Tessa, kissing her and her mother by turns. Serena's heart felt tight and her eyes became hot, a certain sign that tears of joy were about to erupt—again. In this maternal state, she cried over everything—most of it happy, and the rest of it still part of the life she loved.

Andrew glanced at her just as the first tear fell. He bent and kissed it away, smiling down at her before lowering his head to touch her lips once more. Then he moved Tessa between them again and linked arms with Serena as they held each other in a tight group hug. A circle of love. A circle of blessings.

*   *   *   *   *

Dear Reader,

I started writing my debut novel, *A Blessed Life*, when my own heart needed healing. Like Serena, I have a daughter who lives with juvenile rheumatoid arthritis. I experienced some of the same guilt and hopelessness Serena feels and a similar joy when my child began to thrive. Also like Serena, I have struggled with giving up control to God.

I hope you enjoyed meeting the members of Hickory Ridge Community Church as much as I enjoyed creating them. Some of my favorite memories are from growing up as part of a large church family. Because these characters live on in my thoughts, I hope to meet them again in a future story.

Dana Corbit

Take 2 inspirational love stories FREE!

PLUS get a FREE surprise gift!

Mail to Steeple Hill Reader Service™

In U.S.
3010 Walden Ave.
P.O. Box 1867
Buffalo, NY 14240-1867

In Canada
P.O. Box 609
Fort Erie, Ontario
L2A 5X3

YES! Please send me 2 free Love Inspired® novels and my free surprise gift. After receiving them, if I don't wish to receive anymore, I can return the shipping statement marked cancel. If I don't cancel, I will receive 3 brand-new novels every month, before they're available in stores! Bill me at the low price of $3.99 each in the U.S. and $4.49 each in Canada, plus 25¢ shipping and handling and applicable sales tax, if any*. That's the complete price and a saving of over 10% off the cover prices—quite a bargain! I understand that accepting the books and gift places me under no obligation ever to buy any books. I can always return a shipment and cancel at any time. Even if I never buy another book from Steeple Hill, the 2 free books and the surprise gift are mine to keep forever.

103 IDN DNU6
303 IDN DNU7

Name	(PLEASE PRINT)	
Address	Apt. No.	
City	State/Prov.	Zip/Postal Code